THE HANGMAN'S DAUGHTER
AND OTHER STORIES

By the same author

The Young Visiters

Love and Marriage
(with Angela Ashford)

The Hangman's Daughter

and other stories

DAISY ASHFORD

with an introduction by
MARGARET STEEL

Oxford   New York

OXFORD UNIVERSITY PRESS

1983

Oxford University Press, Walton Street, Oxford OX2 6DP

London Glasgow New York Toronto
Delhi Bombay Calcutta Madras Karachi
Kuala Lumpur Singapore Hong Kong Tokyo
Nairobi Dar es Salaam Cape Town
Melbourne Auckland
and associates in
Beirut Berlin Ibadan Mexico City Nicosia

British Library Cataloguing in Publication Data
Ashford, Daisy d. 1972
The hangman's daughter, and other stories.—
(Oxford paperbacks)
I. Title
823'.912[F]   PR6001. S44
ISBN 0-19-281403-6

Printed in Great Britain by
Richard Clay (The Chaucer Press) Ltd.
Bungay, Suffolk

FOREWORD

THE first story in this book, "The Life of Father McSwiney", is published here for the first time. It is the earliest work by Daisy Ashford that survives: family tradition has it that she was only four when she dictated it to her parents. The other two stories were her last. They first appeared in 1920 in *Daisy Ashford: Her Book*, described on its title page as "A Collection of the Remaining Novels by the Author of 'The Young Visiters' together with 'The Jealous Governes,' by Angela Ashford." ("The Life of Father McSwiney" was not in Daisy's possession at this time, which may explain why it was not included.) *The Young Visiters*—"Viseters" is the manuscript spelling—had appeared in 1919, with legendary success.

These were the contents of *Her Book*:

A Short Story of Love and Marriage
The True History of Leslie Woodcock
Where Love Lies Deepest
The Hangman's Daughter
The Jealous Governes *or* The Granted Wish

The first two of these, and the last (the only surviving work by Daisy's sister Angela), were reissued in Oxford Paperbacks in 1982, under the title *Love and Marriage*, with an introduction by Humphrey Carpenter in which he briefly tells the Ashfords' own suitably romantic family story, recounts the discovery and publication of *The Young Visiters*, and looks at the stories themselves with an appreciative critical eye. Daisy's elder daughter, Mrs. Margaret Steel, fills out his account of the Ashford history in her charming introduction to the present volume.

Foreword

Here is what Daisy herself had to say about her last two stories in a Preface to *Her Book*:

" 'Where Love Lies Deepest' was written when I was twelve, and dedicated to our governess of whom I was very fond.

" 'The Hangman's Daughter,' started at the age of about thirteen and finished the following year, I always consider the greatest literary achievement of my youth, for the reason that I put so much more effort into it than any of the others. By this time I had really determined to become an authoress (an ambition which entirely left me after my school days), and I put solid work into 'The Hangman's Daughter' and really tried to write well. I shall never forget my feeling of shock when I read it aloud to my brothers and they laughed at the trial scene! A great friend of mine whose Christian name was Helen, was the heroine (Helen Winston) of this story. She was a little younger than I was, but was far more 'grown-up' in every way, a fact of which I was secretly rather 'jellus,' and it did not require much imagination on my part to picture what she would be at nineteen. I told her she was to be the heroine of my new novel, which I truly thought would thrill *anyone*, and I must say she was as excited as I could have wished. She will be amused now when she reads this book!"

Whether Helen was indeed amused history does not relate: it is hard to believe otherwise. "At all events," as Humphrey Carpenter puts it, " nothing more was to appear from the pen of Daisy Ashford . . . until she died in January 1972, at the age of ninety, having enjoyed the distinction of being a celebrated author whose last work was composed at the age of thirteen." She did once, in adulthood, begin writing her autobiography —but she tore it up without finishing it. Margaret Steel's introduction helps to fill the gap.

CONTENTS

INTRODUCTION

In 1881 the seventh of April fell on Easter Sunday, auspiciously for the Ashford family of Petersham in Surrey. There at the house known as Elm Lodge, where Dickens was reputed to have written *Nicholas Nickleby*, the occupants awaited the birth of the baby who would be the first child of William Ashford, the sixth of his wife Emma—and my mother. A few days later, according to the custom of the Catholic Church, to which Emma belonged, the baby was taken to be baptized, and given the names Margaret Mary Julia— names seldom to be used again because on the day of her christening her youngest half-brother had woven a daisy chain for her to wear during the ceremony, so that ever afterwards she was known as Daisy. Daisy Ashford. Not long afterwards her parents left Grandmother Ashford's house, and moved to Park Gate, a lovely old house in the same village, and here Vera and Angela Ashford were born.

Mr. Ashford spent a lot of his time composing church music, and wrote articles for the Catholic Truth Society, of which he was a founder member. He also had one book published, entitled *Our Waterways*, which he wrote with his friend Urquart Forbes. The talents of

Mrs. Ashford, who had the reputation of being a great wit, lay in a much lighter vein. She wrote and produced with great success a pantomime in rhyme, and after giving a fancy-dress ball wrote and had printed a booklet of limericks describing all the guests. The Ashfords, indeed, might be described as a highbrow and a lowbrow.

Daily letters, the keeping of journals, and reading out loud were all part of family life. In this atmosphere it was not considered at all unusual when Daisy, who could not write quickly enough to express her thoughts, asked her father if she could dictate her first stories to him. With characteristic patience he gladly fell in with this, but he was a stern critic. On one occasion when Daisy was dictating her latest effort to him, he stopped her abruptly, and told her that she had thinly disguised and embroidered the plot of a book she had recently had read to her, and that if she was going to write, the ideas must be her own. It was a lesson she never forgot.

There were two reasons for the family's move to Lewes in 1889. First of all Daisy was considered to be in grave danger of becoming unbearably spoilt by her Aunt Julia, a maiden lady, who after the death of Grandmother Ashford went off to live in nearby Byam Cottage. Daisy was the apple of her eye, and in her view above criticism. The other thing was that people in the house were always becoming ill, and without further investigation this was blamed on the drains of the house, a notion Daisy was to make good use of when she wrote *The Young Visiters*.

Southdown House, as it was renamed by my grandmother, was large and ugly, but for all that a very happy place, and it was here that Daisy set about becoming an author in earnest. Her most treasured possession was a green writing-desk which had pride of place in the nursery. Sitting at this, oblivious to the games played by her younger sisters, which often ended in violent arguments, Daisy created her immortal characters. As she told J. M. Barrie, whom she went to see after he had agreed to write the Preface to *The Young Visiters*, " I adored writing and used to pray for bad weather, so that I need not go out but could stay in and write."

The children were now having regular lessons with their governess, so discipline had to take a firmer hand than hitherto. Mrs. Ashford could be quite stern with her daughters, quelling them with a look known in the family as " Mother's Palm Sunday face ". No one would have dreamt of arguing with her. But it was characteristic of her to bend the rules, and a beautiful day would send her hurrying to the nursery to order a long health-giving walk over the Downs, causing much frustration to the current governess if she happened to be very conscientious—but delight if she did not. Although the family had an adequate number of servants, the children were expected to make their own beds: the heaving of sheets and blankets and the turning of mattresses were considered good for the figure. A reclining board was another feature of the nursery. Deportment was very important. This was a policy which paid dividends, my mother remaining very upright throughout a life which spanned ninety years.

At this stage the Ashford family lived a quite self-contained and very simple life. An excursion to the theatre in Brighton was a terrific treat, and the annual holiday in the Isle of Wight greatly looked forward to, as were return visits to Petersham to stay with Aunt Julia. Here the Ashfords renewed acquaintance with Nanna, the family nurse who had devotedly nursed Daisy through an almost fatal attack of measles at the age of two. Nanna was an intensely disagreeable and autocratic old lady, but the family were so grateful to her that she became Julia Ashford's general factotum, remaining with her until Julia's death, when Daisy travelled with her to Ireland to return her to her relatives.

Where then did Daisy look for her inspiration? To the eyes of a child her parents' life must have seemed to hold all the elements of romance, although in fact parts of it were extremely grim. Emma Walker was born to a life of ease, and she was naturally extravagant. Her father was a rich Nottinghamshire landowner who became even richer when coal was found on his estate. His wife seems to have been rather a remote figure, and we know little of her. Emma had one brother, to whom she was devoted, often extricating him from the scrapes he was adept at getting himself into. Her great occupation was hunting, and she was reputed to have had a marvellous seat. She became engaged to an eligible peer but broke this off to marry a penniless young man in the Hussars, of whom, needless to say, her family strongly disapproved. They lived mostly in Ireland, where Emma, who must have had cause for deep thought, decided to become a Catholic.

Her husband's untimely death brought her back to England, where she was faced with the bleak prospect of bringing up and educating three sons and two daughters. Owing to the intricacies of her father's will she had been disinherited, and the brother to whom she had shown so much loyalty did not reciprocate it. Why she chose to settle in Petersham I do not know, but it was here that she met the parish priest who brought about an introduction between herself and William Ashford.

William, then in middle age, seemed settled in his ways. He had been educated at Eton, and although his family lived very comfortably in a substantial house, they were not rich in the sense that Emma's family had been. His life was orderly and calm, and he was devoted to his mother and sister. Apart from a journey to Rome, he does not seem to have travelled very far. Emma with her exuberant nature must have seemed like a breath of fresh air, and William surely succumbed to her magnetic charm. It certainly could not have been her beauty which bowled him over, though she did have the most beautiful hair. (Hair figures prominently in Daisy's descriptions of her heroines.) Their ultimate marriage, which proved to be a very happy one, began with a honeymoon on which they were accompanied by Emma's youngest son Raymond, known to the family as Baa. He was Daisy's favourite brother.

They were an unconventional family. The elder sisters were allowed much more freedom than was usual at this period, and were often unchaperoned, which would have raised a few eyebrows. Emma, too, never managed to control her extravagant nature, so there were periods of financial embarrassment, during which a picture or a piece of jewellery might disappear. I

have in my possession a miniature painted by my grand-
father which is a copy of a Hoppner that sadly had to be
sold on one such occasion.

There were often visitors to Southdown House,
many of them the young friends of Emma's first family.
I feel sure that they were surreptitiously scrutinized by
Daisy; indeed, she probably used as a literary source any
situation in which she found herself. The quiet little
girl who sometimes accompanied her mother or aunt on
their afternoon calls would have been making a mental
note of the snippets of gossip that she heard, and observ-
ing the manners and mannerisms of the people whom
she met.

Her eldest half-brother Ernest Langley was for a
time on the stage; according to a scrap-book kept by my
grandmother, he got quite good notices. It is highly
probable that some of the leading ladies in these produc-
tions would have been guests at Southdown House.
This would have been a golden opportunity for Daisy,
and I am sure that they unwittingly became the proto-
types for some of the heroines of her stories.

The butler at Southdown House was an Italian, who
had come to the Ashfords as the result of a letter in
which he applied for the post, saying of himself, " All
that you give me, I do love; all that you tell me, I can
do." One evening during a party given by Mrs.
Ashford, Leland, another son, who had a beautiful
trained baritone voice, was entertaining the guests with
an Italian song. Someone crossing the hall found
Alfredo sitting on the stairs in floods of tears; when
asked what the matter was, he replied with true Italian

sentimentality, " Ah he sing Italian! " He possibly
became either Procurio or Francis Minnit in *The
Young Visiters*.

It was surely not entirely coincidence that Lord
Beaufort, who married Gladys in " The Hangman's
Daughter ", lived in Portman Square. I have a bundle
of letters written between 1822 and 1826 by the
Duchess of Roxburgh to her kinsman W. K. Ashford,
my great-grandfather. She writes from Portman Square
—evidently her town house. The letters abound with
the gossip of the day. In one she says, " Town is very
full, and our poor king has been showing himself to
gratify the people. The Levee was very full. Mr.
Tollemache was there he thought His Majesty looked
pale, and no wonder being much fatigued."

Food was very important to the young children, and
often mentioned by Daisy in her stories. Nursery fare
was plain and wholesome: porridge one morning, bread
and milk the next. Tea was just piles of bread and
butter, and sometimes for a treat a halfpenny currant-
bun. A birthday of course produced an iced cake. To
be allowed downstairs for luncheon was the greatest
treat, slightly marred if the older children were there as
they were inclined to favour milk puddings instead of
the more exciting things the younger ones were longing
to partake of. Once Daisy managed to smuggle a menu
out of a restaurant, and used it in the chapter where
Mulberry Beaufort gives his dinner party.

An avid reader, Daisy had a penchant for boys'
stories. *The Fifth Form at St. Dominic's* was a great
favourite and often quoted. She read all the usual

children's books of the period. I remember such titles as *Deb and the Duchess* (by L. T. Meade), Florence Montgomery's *Misunderstood, Rosamond* and *The Purple Jar* by Maria Edgeworth, and Oliver Wendell Holmes's *The Autocrat of the Breakfast Table*. They were mostly of a highly moral character. I think Daisy was once caught red-handed reading a copy of *The Yellow Book*, which was considered very fast, and was probably hidden by her brothers. But my feeling is that she wasn't influenced so much by what she read as by the people around her.

They were a very devoted family and a very jolly one. Angela was certainly her mother's favourite child and, although it was not so evident, Vera was her father's. Daisy was well aware of the situation, but it was one that she accepted without animosity. All her life she was a great peacemaker. After a family row, the butler was heard to murmur in an undertone, " We all know Miss Daisy is the best for all." A visitor to the house once aptly dubbed the children Daisy the Delightful, Vera the Vivacious, and Angela the Angelic.

The family were all staunch Catholics, whose lives revolved round the Church. (Mr. Ashford's mother and sister were always Catholics, but he himself did not become a Catholic until after his coming of age. It was quite usual in those days for the sons to take their fathers' and the daughters their mothers' religion—a system which, because of the climate of the time, was allowed, but not really approved of, by the Catholic Church.) Going to church was never a penance, and Daisy and her sisters were intensely interested in all that happened there. They avidly followed all the events of the liturgical year, so that it was quite natural for Daisy to mention various pious practices in her stories.

Such practices dominate " The Life of Father McSwiney ", which must have been one of the earliest stories Daisy dictated, certainly the earliest in existence. My aunt Vera, who gave me the manuscript, thought it had been composed when Daisy was four. On the face of it, this does seem incredible, and I suppose must remain questionable. On the other hand, a letter survives, dictated by Daisy to her mother shortly after her third birthday, which though it is certainly childish does show a good command of English. Who is to say what she might not have been capable of a year and more later?

The story was based (loosely!) on what Daisy knew of the life of a Jesuit friend of her father's from Lancashire, whose name was indeed James McSwiney (pronounced ' McSweeney '). Father McAuliffe, one of the other priests in the story, was really the parish priest of the Church of St. Pancras in Lewes. A very holy old man, he was loved by everyone. The Irish stable-boys used to vie with one another for the honour of cleaning his boots.

Priests, too, often came to stay, and probably made a point of talking to the children; nor was the Pope a remote figure to Daisy, but someone absolutely real. Her brothers were being educated by monks, but undoubtedly enjoyed the pleasures of life when they returned home for the holidays; so Daisy would have seen no good reason why the Pope and Father McSwiney should not do the same.

During the years at Southdown House, Daisy became aware of abject poverty. She told me of two occasions that made a lasting impression on her. She once witnessed a pathetic old couple parting in the road, each going to a separate workhouse. The second incident occurred when she accompanied her mother on a round of Christmas visits to the poor of the parish. In one cottage there was not a vestige of heating or crumb of food. Of course my grandmother remedied this, but Daisy never forgot it. She hated to hear of people being described as common, and seldom used the expression herself, preferring the word " mere ", which doubled for " ordinary " as well. She always had an affinity to the working classes, and as a child felt they had much more freedom than she did. She hated always having to be accompanied by a nurse or a governess.

The children invented their own games, the only toys they possessed being large families of dolls, each doll endowed with a name and distinctive personality. Vera and Angela's dolls belonged to the nobility: Vera was a duchess, Angela a viscountess, and the dolls had their appropriate titles. Daisy preferred to be poor Mrs. Ham who eked out a living by taking in washing.

There was always a plentiful supply of books, writing materials, and, in the case of Vera, paints. Vera was the artist of the family and produced a lurid poster for the only play Daisy wrote. It was called " A Woman's Crime ", and was performed in the nursery. On this occasion they were honoured by the presence of two real actors, one of whom was O. B. Clarence.

The children's lessons with their governess were

augmented by their father, who taught them Latin and history. Vera was particularly interested in the Indian Mutiny, and would discuss this at length with him. But it was thought that the time had come for something more formal, and together with their great friends Helen and Violet Ballard (Helen was the model for Helen in "The Hangman's Daughter") and an amusing child, Katie Jickling, the daughter of the Anglican vicar, they formed a class which was presided over by a Miss Mabel Smythe. Though unqualified she was the perfect teacher and the children progressed remarkably well with her.

At the time Daisy wrote "Where Love Lies Deepest" she was obviously becoming very interested in fashion and the possibility of travel. As she says herself, this story was dedicated to her governess, of whom she was very fond. I know that at one time she had an Irish governess, who could conceivably have come from a farming background; so it is quite probable that the Langton family were modelled on that of this governess.

At the age of thirteen Daisy considered that she was a real author and started to plan her next novel, "The Hangman's Daughter". She put a great deal of effort into it, and it took her a whole year to write. She was not a little proud of the result. If the Ashfords had thought in terms of careers for their daughters, they might at this point have encouraged Daisy to keep her nose to the grindstone, but of course such an idea did not enter their heads.

It was at this juncture that life was interrupted by

the announcement that Daisy was to go away to a proper school. She was overjoyed at the prospect, and off she went to the Priory, a delightful convent at Haywards Heath, to be joined later by Vera and Angela. The enthusiasm with which she had tackled her writing was now diverted into the ramifications of school life. She loved her time there and remained a loyal Old Girl all her life.

So what happened to Daisy Ashford, the little girl who, to use a modern idiom, had everything going for her? Why did her parents not foresee the bright future which could have been hers, and what of her own feelings?

Her parents certainly did not regard Daisy's talents as anything out of the ordinary, and they did not produce her works for all and sundry to exclaim over. After all, Vera and Angela were equally talented. Vera was artistic enough to be sent at a later date to the Slade, and Angela, besides her literary prowess, was extremely musical. Both of them, too, spent much time writing for pleasure.

The period after Daisy left school must have been very dull. Lewes was not the most exciting place in which to live, and her new-found leisure may have fallen rather flat. Sadly, the urge to write left her, although her talent never did. Her letters were a joy to all who received them. I particularly remember her wartime letters, in which she described her activities in the village. She would write of some trivial event, which probably hardly anyone else was aware of, and it became immensely funny. She was equally good at telling stories. " Do tell us a story " was a frequent cry of my youth. She invented whole families, and our animals always had special voices. One large tom-cat we had was always known as The Butler, and his timid mother as The Widow.

It was some years later that Daisy prevailed upon her parents to allow her to take a secretarial course in London, where Vera was already enjoying life at the Slade. This was all rather against the conventions of the time, but quite in keeping with Mrs. Ashford's character. Daisy shared Vera's studio just off the Fulham Road, where they had the greatest fun, meeting many of the up-and-coming artists of the day. One of the highlights of their time there was The Chelsea Arts Ball. There would have been plenty of material here, if Daisy had cared to use it. It seems that she could only cope with one enthusiasm at a time.

Daisy was a very shy and diffident person, seldom at her best with strangers. Her meeting with Barrie was a great disappointment. He was equally shy and there seems to have been a kind of impasse between them, but with her family and the people she knew well she really sparkled.

She was very unworldly in the sense that money and possessions were unimportant to her, which is probably why she ended her life with little of either. Nor did position worry her, and she married entirely for love. People and their feelings were what mattered to her most. During the latter part of her life, when some of her stories were republished and *The Young Visiters* was made into a play, I saw her being interviewed by many journalists and television personalities. Some were visibly puzzled by the shy, rather vague old lady, who although she had reputedly made a lot of money seemed to have ended up in quite humble circumstances. I think that those who knew and loved her books were probably expecting someone much more scintillating, and those who did not or had only given them a cursory glance on the train from London were even more non-plussed. For them she remained a complete enigma.

I wonder whether, if she had continued to write, she would as she became more proficient have relegated her earlier stories to the waste-paper basket, so depriving the world of so much fun. I am glad that she stopped when she did.

The Life of Father McSwiney

PART I

HIS CHILDHOOD

On the twenty-fourth of June in the year 1830 James McSwiney was born in Cork at the south of Ireland. His mother and father already had some girls, the eldest of whom was thirteen and a half, and, as this was their first boy, they said he should be brought up as a Jesuit priest. James McSwiney, even when he was a baby, seemed to have a saintly smile on his Jesuit-like face, and, as his mother watched him in his cradle, she said to herself, " He shall and must be a priest." So when he was going to be christened his mother put a white ribbon round his neck to remind her to ask the priest something about his being a Jesuit.

The priest said, just after the christening, " This boy is very saintly, I am glad he is called James."

As he grew older, his mother looked upon him as one for his sisters to take example by. One day, when he was seven years old, he went in to his mother full of a grand and Jesuit-like joy.

" What is it James? " said his mother.

" Oh," said the little saint, " I've been talking to a lady who says she is the mistress of the Catholic School, and she wanted to know if I might go to the Catholic School. I hope you will let me; I should like to learn the Catechism."

So his mother said he might go. When he went to the school on Sunday, the mistress asked him if he had made his confession.

" No," said little James, " but I should like to so much, as I feel rather wicked."

" Well, I will ask the priest to hear you this evening. He will give you plentiful instructions, as he is a great friend of your father's."

" Oh thank you so much ! " said little James ; and he worked on much better with his Catechism.

So that evening, after he had spoken some saintly words to one of his companions, he went to make his confession to the gallant priest ; and after two other people had made their confessions, he crept silently into the confessional for the first time. He pulled back the curtain, as he had seen the others do, and meekly and quickly told his sins, and the priest gave him a long absolution, as he was so saintly.

After he had gone out of the confessional, the priest was perfectly struck with this boy ; so he told the people he had no more time to hear confessions, and came out after James, to see how different he was from other people. He was just saying his penance when the priest's holy hand touched his face.

" How is it you are so good ? " whispered the priest.

" I did not know I was so much more good than other people, but I hope I am."

" Well, I think you are, my good boy," said the sympathizing priest.

After this the priest asked James if he would

4

like to have some supper with him in the Presbytery.

" Thank you, Father Cullen," said James, " I must say, if it is the first time in my life, I *am* hungry."

When Father Cullen and James McSwiney were seated at the table, Father Cullen said, " My dear little boy ! I think I know something that will please you. There is going to be a very grand confirmation in this church, and although you have only just made your first confession it will be a holy and nice thing to be confirmed by the precise Bishop, who is rather old—but no matter."

James fairly fainted away with joy. " Bless my heart, soul, and mind ! " he said, " the thing I have wished for all my life."

The priest grinned under his table napkin, but said nothing. " Jolly, holy little chap ! " he mumbled, in a stubborn sort of way. That night, when James McSwiney went home, little he knew the impression he had left on the priest's heart, through his holy apostolic ways.

When the priest that night laid his scurfy head on the pillow, he could not help mumbling, and shutting his watery eyes, because of the holy James. He also blew his nose two or three times, which he very seldom did.

When James McSwiney got home to his mother, she asked him where he had been. He said, in a serious and solemn tone, that he had been with Father Cullen, talking about a confirmation.

The mother spoke rather crossly to James, for the first time in her life.

"Why, you've not made your first confession yet," said his mother; for she didn't know that James had made it.

"Yes, but I have made it, Mother," said he, coughing violently, for he had got the croup.

When James McSwiney went to bed that night, after heaving eaten one pancake, it suddenly entered his head that he did not know where the confirmation was going to be. So the next morning he got up about one o'clock, and he put on his brown dressing-gown, and he tied a red silk sash round his waist, and then, putting on a pair of very holey stockings, and his new dressing-slippers, and a new sailor hat, he crept out of his bedroom door.

He went down on to the second landing, where a little brown mahogany cupboard stood; it belonged to James. He turned the silver key and, looking on the middle shelf, he produced, from a black tin box, a beautiful ivory-backed hairbrush wrapped in tissue-paper. He slipped it into the pocket of his dressing-gown, and then he went down the kitchen stairs, and out at the back door, where some very "smelly" potatoes had been thrown. Then he hurried down the street, dressed as he was, meaning to go to the Presbytery.

When he got there, he knew it was no use to ring the bell, for the fat old housemaid was sure to be in bed at this hour. The door wasn't locked, so he went up to the priest's bedroom and, turning the golden handle, went in. When he got in, Father Cullen was just getting out of bed, and shuffling about in his cotton night-shirt.

"Hullo, James!" he said, at the top of his voice.

James shuddered a little, but he came forward and kissed the priest. The priest put his bare legs into bed again, and James, after seating himself at the foot of the bed, began to wish the Priest good morning.

After the priest had looked at James a few minutes, he noticed that he was only dressed in his night-clothes. The priest pulled his bell as hard as he could, and up came the fat house-maid, who had only just buttoned up her muslin frock, which had burst a little at the sleeves; but up she came, and was surprised to see James there.

"One poached egg on a plate, and a cup of milk," screamed the priest, "and have it ready in five minutes."

James by this time was feeling rather cold, and he tied his pocket handkerchief tightly round his neck, and then looked the priest full in the face. The priest too was rather puzzled as to whether he should lie in bed and not

7

get up at all, or send poor little James home again.

Soon the fat housemaid came up and plumped the egg down on the bed, and spilled half the milk over the priest's head.

" I wish you would not do that ! " said the priest, scratching his head violently with his elbow, which was rather bony.

After James had eaten the egg, and drunk the drop of milk that was left, he jumped down off the bed, and patted the priest. Father Cullen fairly didn't know what to do. He opened his eyes, and sat up in bed, and after catching several fleas he told James he was a good little boy.

The priest very soon got up and dressed himself, and then asked James if he would like some breakfast, though it was only half past five in the morning. James nodded his head, and a liquid smile came over his face.

As soon as James had finished his breakfast, he took out a clean pocket handkerchief from his pocket, and spread it on the window sill. He then took out from his pocket the ivory brush.

" Jingo ! " said the priest under his breath, for he thought it very lovely.

" Look here ! " said James, gazing at the priest, who was standing sideways, " if you will promise on your word of honour to tell me what day the confirmation is, and what name I ought to take, and give me full instructions, I will give you the beautiful brush. See! it brushes lovely," said he, smoothing down his back hair.

The priest took the brush out of the boy's hand, and pressed his hand flat on the bristles, and said it was very nice, and thanked James.

" How old are you? " said Father Cullen, looking at James with an expression on his face that evidently didn't agree with him, or he would not have turned as sick as he did.

" I am seven and two months," said James with an air.

" Oh! bless us," said the priest under his breath, " I don't know what I can do, because they don't allow you to be confirmed unless you are nine years old."

" Oh! that the years would only pass quicker," said James, bending in homage on one knee.

" I know then what I will do," said the priest, bringing from behind the curtain a little pot of water. " I will get out my paintbox and brush, and I will paint ' Nine and a half ' on your chest in black figures."

" But then, I won't be confirmed with a bare chest," said James, looking very much astonished at the priest's conduct.

" Not exactly," said the priest, smoothing down his middle-parting, and touching his " biscuit "; " you will have a pocket handkerchief put all round you except where the ' Nine

9

and a half ' is painted: then that will show, and they will think it is your real age."

About three weeks after this eventful day, the Grand Confirmation was to be held in the Catholic church, which was done up with white satin and white lilies of the valley. Poor little James McSwiney was cautiously tied to a seat with a white silk ribbon till it was his turn to be confirmed; and in the midst of his tears he heard that one of the girls took the name of Violet—he didn't in the least know why.

At last his turn came: but as he was untied he was whispered to by his most unkind mother, that he would be tied again directly he came back. When he knelt down at the feet of the Bishop, the Bishop winked his eyes, to make sure that he saw the " Nine and a half " on his chest. James wondered very much why he was not confirmed as quickly as the other children.

After this Sam (as the Bishop's name was called) flipped some balsam at the " Nine and a half ", so as to make sure that it was not a seal of piety that the child had had left to him by some of his forefathers. The Bishop then scraped it with his short nail, to see if it would come off, but finding it would not, he began to confirm him. James took the name of Samson, because he was atrociously strong for his age.

PART II

HIS JESUIT LIFE

WHEN James McSwiney was about twenty-five, he began to be a novice for the Jesuit life. After he had left off being a novice, he took two or three vows, and these are they: first, " I will try not to be wicked "; second, " I will go to confession twice a week "; third, " I will never commit any culpable ignorance of the doctrines of the Church."

After he had taken his vows, he began to wear horsehair shirts, and very tight belts with gold buttons. He wore sandals half a size too large for him, and a floppy hat with a green band, to show he was a Jesuit. He bought himself a magnificent prayer-book the day before he went to the monks' college.

When he got there, a housemaid in a red frock came out and said, " You must be very quiet, Jesuit! for there are visitors. There are four priests, and two very ignorant bishops."

He was then led to a dear little sitting-room, in which he found a first-rate novel which he began to read.

In a few minutes a man cook came in, and announced that there was a holy priest named Father McAuliffe come to see the Jesuit. Then little thin Father McAuliffe came walking in on his little thin wiry legs. Father McAuliffe went piously over to Father McSwiney, and said that he had come from Lewes. I will now describe this most valuable priest.

He had tinged curly hair, brushed back, and

coming over one eye. He had most expressive pale blue eyes, which looked as if he had just come a very long journey, and a tender mouth. He had about sixteen teeth of pure white, and a sweet early French nose. He was most tall and angelic, and as he walked in he looked like an uncanonized saint.

"How do you do, my dear Father McAuliffe," exclaimed Father McSwiney.

"I do very well, thank you," replied Father McAuliffe, in a sweet angelic voice.

"I expect", said the good fat Father McSwiney, as he sat down, "you will be a canon in a few days, you look so dreadfully pious."

"Oh! well I don't quite know," said Father McAuliffe.

Then Father McSwiney blew his nose and began thus: "You know, I said the Mass of St. Bernard this morning, and I don't think it agreed with me very much, as I don't feel very well."

"I am so sorry to hear that," began Father McAuliffe, rapidly shrinking as he was not very strong; "it seems a great pity that a novice should not agree with his mass."

"It does seem a pity," said Father McSwiney, "but I never had a great devotion to St. Bernard."

"I am afraid", said Father McAuliffe, looking very sad and timid, "that my Mission is very small, and somehow I'm rather uneasy about it."

14

" Is that so ? " said Father McSwiney; " if I could convert a duke or two and send them down to you, that might make it better, mightn't it ? "

" It would be so very kind if you would," said Father McAuliffe, " you see I don't quite know how to arrange my services. I have confessions before and after mass every morning, but the people tell so very few sins that the absolution isn't so long; so I can't sit peacefully there, and think over what vestment I shall wear; and in my sermons I really don't know what to say; I either talk about the birth of our Lord, or obedience to the commandments of the Church, and I am sure the people must have heard it all before."

" That reminds me ", said Father McSwiney, " that I have had three sermons given to me by Father Seraphim, and they are all written out; they might do—you could read them out on the three coming Sundays. By that time, perhaps, the monk will have given me some more, which I will send to you, as I am not in need of them at all."

" It would be such a pleasure if you would send me two or three," answered Father McAuliffe; " I'm sure I will be most grateful to you, and I will say many Our Fathers and Hail Marys for you. I suppose I had better go and see the priest of this retreat place. I have business to talk with him, if you do not mind my leaving you."

" Well to tell the truth, I am coming with you," said Father McSwiney, with a chuckle in his chest.

Then the two Fathers rose, and walked up some china stairs.

" You are lucky, holy Father," said a novice to Father McSwiney as he passed by.

" I know not the reason then," answered Father McSwiney, going upstairs.

At last he reached a small room, in which sat the Pope, holding the habit which Father McSwiney did not know he was just going to receive.

" I have brought you a habit," said Pius IX, holding out a brown habit with a hood to it.

" Thank you, dear Pope," said Father McSwiney, throwing himself at the feet of Pope Pius IX.

Five days later Father McSwiney knocked at the Pope's door.

" Come in," said the Pope in an ill voice.

" You have given me the wrong habit," said the good Jesuit.

" Have I? I thought you were going to be of the First Order of St. Francis," said the mild and innocent Pius IX.

" Please give me the black habit, if your holiness does not mind," answered the most " beautiful-in-his-words " Father McSwiney.

" Most willingly," answered the Pope, giving the black habit at that moment to the Jesuit.

16

" My most honoured thanks to you," and out went Father McSwiney.

A retreat at Manresa was given by the Revd. T. Gordon Goodwin, and Father McSwiney was shown upstairs by him after having said a pious goodbye to the Holy Father. The room into which he was shown was very small indeed; it was furnished with three chairs and a small table in the middle, on which was the Old Testament and other pious books. In one corner of the room in a very draughty place was a bed made of an old straw mattress covered over with a quilt. Where the fire *ought* to have been, but was not, was a small grotto made of oak wood. On this grotto was a statue of Our Lady with two wax candles each side.

" Here ", said Father Goodwin, " is your room; you see you have everything you want but your bath, and you will find that the opposite side of the landing. Whenever you are in here you must pray hard."

" Certainly I shall be delighted," said the pious Father McSwiney, clasping his hands tight.

" You may do what you like for half an hour," said Father Goodwin; " then I will tell you what you must next do."

After this Father Goodwin left the room, and Father McSwiney began wondering what to do. He took up a book on the table called *Daily Devotions for a Pious Life*. In this he found a large card on which was written the rule of life for those who were to be Jesuits. This is what he read:

At 5 in the morning the rising bell rings. You are given a quarter of an hour to dress in, then the mass bell rings and the novices walk to the church followed by the Holy Father and the Revd. Gordon Goodwin. After that, devotions till half past seven, then breakfast, which lasts for twenty minutes and which is bread and butter and coffee except if it be a fasting day. After breakfast they go for a walk followed by the same two people. The walk is always to Grotto Lane where they say prayers before the grotto for half an hour. Then they go home singing the Litany all the way, which is considered rather smart by the public in the district. When they get home, morning prayers and church service till dinner time, at which the novices are a little bit offended because they want time for novice recreation. Dinner at twelve, for which they have a slice of dry bread and a bloater regularly with a drink of water besides. Then recreation for an hour. During that time all the novices play at pious tableaux, for which the Holy Father lends them an alb or two and some strips of blue linen; Father Goodwin lends a biretta. The Holy Father and Father Goodwin play Nap in the summerhouse or have donkey rides up and down the garden. Then the novices go to the public class-room, where the Holy Father and Father Goodwin read in turns the life of a very good Jesuit. After that a hymn is sung to clear their minds, after which they write a composition on this good Jesuit, and if it is wrong they are allowed to correct it in the garden with the book. At four o'clock tea, which is the same as breakfast and lasts twenty minutes. Then they may write a letter home, which must first be seen by the Holy Father. Then they have a procession round the garden singing the Litany of the Holy Name, after which they go to church for Rosary Sermon and Benediction; then they come home and have supper, which is the same as dinner with a little roast meat added; then they make meditations on the Day of Judgement and other things such as Daniel in the Lions' Den, The Last Supper and the Annunciation. Then recreation for half an hour, during which they run races with the Holy Father and Father Goodwin or else they have a walk in the woods. Then they go again to Grotto Lane and come home by the town. Then they go to bed at 9.30 after having made a second meditation on the Creation. Then they all go to the bathroom and the Holy Father listens outside to hear they don't make any rude observation on the Manresa Retreat. They use either Old Windsor or Pear's soap or Cucumber and Glycerine as a real treat. They then put on a horsehair night-gown and retire to their bedrooms, where they sleep soundly.

Next morning Father McSwiney woke up and was surprised to find that Father Goodwin was calling him rather loudly. He jumped up and had his bath and then the Pope, who was in the dining-room, said that all the novices were to be taken to the meditation room to be tried on piousness.

This is how the Pope began: he said to Father McSwiney, who stood at the top of the class, " Say the Lord's Prayer."

Father McSwiney began in his low voice and after he had finished the Pope said, " What were you thinking about when you said it?"

"God," said Father McSwiney slowly.

"That's all right," said the Pope; "come here to me."

Father McSwiney walked up, his sacred face beaming with joy.

"Pax tecum," exclaimed the Pope, "you are the piousest of all."

Father McSwiney smiled and looked round at the other novices as if to say, "What do you think of that?", at which the other novices were rather insulted.

"I'll make you a Jesuit if you like," exclaimed the Pope.

Father McSwiney said "Yes", and this is how he was made a Jesuit. First of all the Pope washed his face in holy water and oil and then blessed him; after that he gave him fresh clothes and the Jesuit habit.

"Now," said the Pope, "you must stay in this monastery till you have grown a beard and then you will be a Jesuit."

When his beard had grown he felt rather stuffy and wished monks could go without beards. And then a great event was to happen in honour of his being a Jesuit. The Pope invited twenty priests, six bishops and the Arch one, and forty-one ladies and twenty-seven gentlemen who were not clergy, and a lovely mass was to be said at which the ladies were only allowed to sing the *Kyrie*.

When the mass was over a lovely breakfast took place in the Manresa gardens. This is what it consisted of. There was first some lovely Italian coffee which the Pope had brought with him and some French tea, and then in the middle of the whipped creams, as they were eating them, the Pope said, " Let us make speeches—you begin, Father McSwiney."

Father McSwiney got up on a chair and said, " Clergy, ladies and gentlemen, as I have been made a Jesuit I stand on this rickety chair to give you thanks for coming to the entertainment, and I am sorry to say the dear good Pope is going away, so I must turn out of this and go where the kind-hearted Jesuits send me; of course I don't mean to say that I think myself pious because I am a Jesuit—I might be very wicked. Oh how well I remember the first day I was in this monastery "—and here he felt very like crying, so he got off the rickety chair and the Pope gave him a bun and an ice-cream in honour of his nice speech.

Then the Pope made his speech, but he stood on a throne and said, " Dominus vobiscum et cum spiritu tuo in nomine Patris et Filii etc. This is a happy day. I feel cold and joyous and I return thanks to the darling Father McSwiney who is so humble during his speeches—he says he is wicked but ah ! his goodness runs through my heart like sacramental wine."

Here the Pope began to weep violently and

nobody knew what for, but he managed to get off his throne somehow, and the Archbishop lugged him into an armchair as he thought he was going to faint, and two bishops poured wine down his throat.

As soon as he stopped weeping he jumped up and said in a pathetic voice, " Just one dance please before I go ", and the ladies, six or seven of them, rushed to be his partner.

As so many wished to be his partner he would not dance but ordered the other people to, and two bishops played a duet on a piano which they had been learning for a long while. The Pope laughed a great deal and drank several glasses of champagne. Father McAuliffe was there and danced a little but he was too nervous to go on. He did not drink any champagne as he was afraid it might turn his head.

The next day, as Father McSwiney was reading the New Testament in his room, in walked the Pope all ready dressed in his vestments.

" Hullo Father ! " he said; " I am off to see the London sights, and I mean to take you with me. Have you packed ? " he added with a sigh of relief.

" I am very very sorry, Your Holiness," replied Father McSwiney, " but I did not expect such a grand invitation as this."

" All right," answered the Pope, " you pack

up while I put up a few new shirts in my box which have just unexpectedly come."

Father McSwiney, in a great state of excitement, bundled up his monkish clothes into his portmanteau and walked downstairs with it in his hand, and continued to wait till the Holy Father would appear.

" I'm coming," shouted the Pope from the top of the stairs, " and I will pay your fare."

As soon as Father McSwiney and the Pope had bid a tearful goodbye to their sympathizing companions, they soon found themselves walking hand in hand into the station at Barnes. After having tried their weight, and taken a piece of chocolate from the slot, they soon found themselves seated in a first-class carriage and going off to London.

" The first thing we'll do, you know," said the Pope, " is to go to the Opera: it's very good, I've heard them say."

" Ah! I daresay," said Father McSwiney smiling, " but that is not in my line."

" Good gracious! " said the Pope in astonishment, " but you'll have to go to Drury Lane."

" That's a deal better! " exclaimed Father McSwiney, " and I heard Father McAuliffe say that in love affairs piety comes in, and it has been my greatest ambition to see a pious love affair."

" Then that's right," said the Pope, getting

out of the train, as they had now arrived in London.

I will now tell you where these two went. They went to Durrant's Hotel to spend a few nights with a favourite Catholic waiter of theirs. The first lark they had was to go to Drury Lane with this waiter.

As the three walked together the waiter said, " There's a love scene in the play ", and here the Pope nudged Father McSwiney.

There was a love scene, and it was very pious, and in it there was a great deal of conversation about St. Joseph, and Father McSwiney laughed with pleasure; in fact the Pope did too.

Between the acts they went out and had brandy and water and a pint of whisky toddy, and the Pope, although the Father of all Christians, thought it was quite necessary to do so.

They did not enjoy Drury Lane as much as they thought they would, because the lady at the bar kissed her hand to Father McSwiney, and that they thought was very fast. So they immediately went to the Gaiety Restaurant to have a few mutton chops and fried soles.

In the middle of supper the Pope rang the bell for some mashed potatoes and gravy, and in came a red-faced tipsy waiter. The Pope was fairly astonished, and to show that he was so he poured two or three drops of water down the waiter's throat, and patted his back to see if

24

it would make him come un-drunk, but it was no good.

So what do you think that talented Father McSwiney did? He made the waiter sit in front of the fire till he got his right senses, and then he sat beside him on the sofa and gave him full instructions on not being drunk, while the Pope looked on and smoked a pipe. After that awful adventure they soon left that restaurant you may be sure.

That night these two were very unfortunate. They could not find a bed anywhere, so they wandered about the low streets of London till they saw a fat old man, who volunteered to give them a night's lodging in his Public . . .

*[Here a third of a page of the
manuscript is torn off and missing]*

. . . was rather . . . they caught the fleas and went to sleep.

The next morning the Pope told Father McSwiney to go and teach in St. Peter's College in Russia, and the good Pope went back to Rome after having had a merry trip, and then he left Father McSwiney with many tears and a little present of a pair of vestments and his photograph. And now Father McSwiney is very comfortable at Manresa where he first began his monkish life.

Where Love Lies Deepest

CHAPTER I

THE silvery moon rises slowly above the mountains of white clouds and sheds its quiet light upon one of the most beautiful scenes of the sheltered nooks in the picturesque county of Devonshire. The tall green hills, so thickly covered with wild thyme rise clear and high against the blue sky above. The rippling waters of a little streamlet glide softly upon its way through lovely banks of sweet green moss. Presently a white cloud envelopes the pale moon and all is darkness !

Only for a moment, the cloud passes away and the bright light pours down upon two figures. The one the tall slim figure of a young girl, the other the broad well built figure of a richly dressed man. He wore a beautifully made blue serge suit and a white tie fastened with a gold and diamond pin. His felt hat fitted as though it had been made for him and his light overcoat and kid gloves were like the rest of his toilet—well made and of a rich material. His black hair grew thickly on his head and his brown eyes glared fiercely, his brown skin was red with rage and his white teeth were clenched.

29

The girl on the contrary was poorly dressed
and did not seem at home in the presence of
the rich man. She wore a pale grey dress
trimmed with green velvet. It had seen its
best days for it was worn in many places. She
wore a straw hat and a white scarf round her
neck. She was a lovely girl ! ! Her plentiful
golden hair was coiled into a knob behind and
cut in a small fringe in front. Her large blue
eyes spoke of many mysteries and were fringed
by golden lashes. Her cherry coloured lips
were small and pressed together in her nervous
state. Her white teeth were clenched and
she trembled under the viscious glare of her
companion.

"I tell you Beatrice you are out of your
senses, you must be, there is no doubt of it,
how can you refuse such an offer"? said the
man fiercely.

"Oh Lawrence do listen to me", said the
unhappy girl, "it is impossible, it cannot be.
You are very kind, and I always had and always
shall have a very great respect for you, but I
cannot marry you, indeed I cannot ! we are no
match, I am poor and you are rich. Besides
I have a reason for not accepting you for my
husband. Oh Lawrence you make me so
unhappy ! " and here the poor girl stopped
short, gave a hurried look round and pressed
her hand to her heart.

"Beatrice Langton you are a lunatic " cried

the man, "give me an answer straight out—
yes or no. Will you be my wife? speak out
and dont go jibbering on in that sentimental
fashion; say yes and you will live in luxury
and riches for the rest of your life, say no and
you go home poor and degraded. Now give
me an answer Yes or No"!

The girl raised her head and spoke thus—
"Lawrence I am very sorry to say it but my
answer is No! Goodbye Mr Cathcart, goodbye Lawrence, perhaps we shall never meet
again. What? you will not even shake hands!
Very well, goodnight Lawrence, goodnight".

She turned and went away leaving him in the
darkness.

CHAPTER II

BEATRICE LANGTON'S HOME

WHEN Beatrice went away she made straight
for her home for it was close on nine and her
mother would be anxious. Her heart was
heavy and her eyelids were wet with fast falling
tears as she made her way across the desolate
moor. Presently she came to the stream and
after crossing the bridge she made for the
common. On the outskirts of the village stood
her home. A little brown cottage with carefully trimmed roses and jasmine creeping up
the porch and a neat little garden in front.

She opened the gate, walked up the path and opened the door.

What a pleasant scene was there before her ! A bright fire was burning in the well kept hearth and an old lady sat beside it knitting stockings for the coming winter. Many pictures adorned the walls. A gentleman was writing at a table in the window. Three little girls all in red frocks and white pinnafores were employed in different ways. The eldest was some ten years old with curly hair and blue eyes and was busy with some cornflowers and poppies in a glass vase. The other two who looked about eight and six, had brown eyes and very fair hair were looking at a book at the middle table. They all jumped up as Beatrice entered.

"Why Beatrice dear how late you are " ! said Mrs. Langton " I sent your supper down. Mary, ring the bell, Beatrice must be hungry."

" No I am not " answered Beatrice smiling wearily and seating herself in the chair her sister had placed for her " I am only very tired and would like to go to bed."

" Oh you must have something ", said Mr. Langton, " Cook made some lovely cheese cakes for supper, and you shall have some wine to drink ".

Just then the maid entered, and in spite of herself Beatrice was soon enjoying a hearty meal.

"Oh there is half past nine"! cried Mrs. Langton, "Lily and Tina go to bed at once, Mary can wait up for Beatrice if she likes".

The two little children ran off hand in hand murmering "lucky Mary".

CHAPTER III

IT was eight o'clock next morning when Beatrice opened her weary eyes and looked round her little room. She jumped up immediately and ran down to breakfast.

Her father had just gone off to his farming, but her mother was sitting in her accustomed place by the fireside reading a letter which was evidently causing her some anxiety.

"Well Mother", cried Beatrice, "what is the matter"?

"Well dear" replied Mrs. Langton sipping her tea as she spoke, "I have had a letter from Mrs. Vindsor who went abroad last year, and she wants you to go and spend the winter with her in Paris. I would like you to go dear, but you are my eldest child and you are by no means strong".

"Oh Mother do let me go, I should enjoy it, and you know I am much stronger since I took to eating Mother Segul's Syrup."

33

" I know my love ", said Mrs. Langton, " I will speak to your father about it, and in the meantime pour me out another cup of tea please ".

Beatrice caught hold of the teapot smiling happily as she did so ; her father was not the man to say no, and what he said her mother seldom differed from ; so she cut her bread and carved her bacon singing a merry song through it all.   After breakfast Beatrice dusted the room, got the children ready for school, and then adjusting a straw hat upon her golden tresses she prepared herself for a saunter through the beautiful fields fresh with the smell of new mown hay and Alderny cows. She gathered flowers as she went and though she felt bright and happy by the news the post had brought there was a sore corner in her heart — she had quarrelled with Lawrence Cathcart, and there was not a man in Senbury Glen who did not know his temper !   As she strolled along she caught sight of Mr. Langton who was discussing the subject of Welsh sheep with a tradesman.   He saw Beatrice and walked towards her.

" Well Bia ", he cried, " looking at my cows ? aren't they lovely ? "

" Beautiful Father ", cried Beatrice, " but do you know Mrs. Vindsor wants me to go to Paris and spend the winter with her family, and may I go " ?

Chapter III

"Yes certainly," said Mr. Langton, "and I suppose that means you would like a pound or two to buy dresses and hats"?

Beatrice bit her lip and smiled, "I suppose so father", she said gazing placidly at her worn elbows.

"Very well," said her father, "I will give you £10. I should advise a blue serge dress and a yellow hat".

"Oh no father"! shrieked Beatrice, "I will get a green dress and a hat trimmed with roses".

"Very well," said Mr. Langton kicking the hay with his feet, "do as you please my dear, by the bye, when are you expected in Paris"?

"Tomorrow week father", said Beatrice, "at least so mother says".

Mr. Langton whistled and then turning to his daughter he said, "I tell you what Bia, you had better call at the dressmaker on your way home, I hate a bustle at the last moment". so saying Mr. Langton gave his daughter £10 in ready gold! Beatrice took them home and put them in her purse till the afternoon when she paid a long visit to the dressmaker. She invested in a lovely green silk dress trimmed with a delicate shade of rose pink, and the dainty little hat was of the same picturesque colours. She likewise bought a costly diamond brooch and two silver bangles to make up the £10

On coming out of the shop she turned on to the moors for a last walk before going to Paris, for there would be plenty to do at home such as darning stockings, mending clothes etc : She called for Nelly Reeves (a friend of hers) ; it would be a good chance to outdo her, thought Beatrice, for Nelly had been to Italy the year before and did nothing but boast of it all day. So the two girls arm in arm started for the moors. Nelly Reeves was a tall good looking girl, slightly pretty, but with none of the wistful beauty about her that was so clearly stamped on all Beatrice Langton's features. She had black hair and what she considered beautiful eyes, though they really were small and vacant in their perpetual stare.

"Well I hope you will enjoy yourself" she remarked briskly when Beatrice told her of the invitation to Paris.

"I am sure I shall," said Beatrice, gently feeling her hair behind, "only think of the delights of it ! The Vindsors live in a Chateau you know" !

"Yes, I suppose it will be jolly for you", said Nelly "who are the Vindsors" ?

"Oh dont you remember Clara Vindsor" ? said Beatrice, "she was so very pretty and polite in her ways".

"I recollect her", said Nelly gazing on the far away blue hills, "oh Beatrice how lovely that view is " !

36

"Yes," said Beatrice sadly, "I came up
here last night for a walk ".

"Alone "? asked Nelly.

Beatrice wished she had not spoken then,
but being frank and straightforward she replied
"no I was not alone."

"Who with " ? inquired Nelly.

"Never mind," retorted Beatrice.

"Oh Beatrice do tell me " coaxed Nelly,
"I'll not tell a soul."

"I dont care if you do," said Beatrice
coldly.

"Well let me see if I can guess " said Nelly
artfully "was it Mr. Cathcart " ?

"What makes you guess him " ? asked
Beatrice angrily.

"Why because he has been paying attentions
to you lately, and I thought he might have
come up here to propose " said Nelly.

"You have most silly ideas " ! retorted
Beatrice, "if you dont leave off please to go
home, what if he did propose " ?

"Oh nothing at all," replied Nelly, "if
you are so disagreable I *will* go home," so saying
Miss Reeves tucked up her dress and walked
home.

"Life is hard " ! sighed Beatrice, "nothing
seems to go right, first I quarrel with Lawrence
and then with Nelly—— why what is that " ?
she cried as she caught sight of something gold
glittering in the pathway.

She stooped to pick it up; it was a gentleman's gold link, beautifully carved and engraved with the initials L.C.

"L.C." repeated Beatrice handling the link pensively "why they are his initials. Can it be his I wonder? why yes" she continued, "here is the name Lawrence Cathcart; His Links! yes they are his, I will keep them and I may some day have occasion to return them to him", so saying she put the articles in her leather purse and turned towards home.

In some unaccountable way Beatrice turned into the High Street and had to pass Lawrence Cathcart's house, a splendid white stone building standing apart from the other houses in a beautiful garden of well tended blooms.

"What riches"! sighed Beatrice pausing at the iron gates, and as her blue eyes searched the lovely grounds her glance fell upon Lawrence Cathcart. He was standing under a tree with an open book in his hands. He wore a light fawn suit and his black curly hair was exposed to the Autumn sun; and as Beatrice gazed on this good looking young man she wondered why she had not noticed before how exquisitely curly his hair and moustache was, how fine his nose and eyes, and how beautifully his mouth was curved.

But she did not talk to him or try to attract his attention, and sad and disheartened she walked home.

CHAPTER IV

TEA was ready when Beatrice returned home and she drew her chair and clustered round the table.

"Well, what is your dress like"? asked Mrs. Langton as she passed the butter to her husband.

"Oh it is lovely Mother" answered Beatrice, "and oh Father" she continued, "I bought some jewellry too"!

"Jewellry," cried Mr. Langton stirring his tea very hard, "with my money"?

"Well, yes father", sighted Beatrice, "I hope you are not angry"?

"What did you buy" enquired Mr. Langton.

"Two bracelets and a brooch" said Beatrice sadly.

Mr. Langton coughed and helped himself to some strawberry jam.

"I have been very busy putting some embroidery on your white petticoat all the afternoon", said Mrs. Langton trying to change the subject, "you know I had a telegram to say you are expected on Thursday instead of next week."

"Oh Mother" said Beatrice, "I must begin to pack at once"!, so saying she flew up to her bedroom, and ten minutes later the floor was littered with as many articles of clothing as you could wish to see, and when Mrs. Langton came up after tea she found her daughter seated on the bed amid stockings of every shade, curling some crimson feathers.

" My dear Beatrice " ! cried that good lady in astonishment, " what are you doing " ?

" Well I was trying to pack mother " answered Beatrice calmly.

" I see " said Mrs. Langton folding up a blue skirt as she spoke, " if you will allow me to help you I think you will manage better ".

" Very well " replied Beatrice " there are the trunks ".

" Yes I see them " said Mrs. Langton, " I think your new dress and hat had better go in the basket trunk dont you " ?

" Perhaps so " said Beatrice gathering the stockings off the bed, " Oh mother, to think that the day after tomorrow I shall be going to Paris " !

" Yes indeed dear " replied Mrs. Langton glancing round the littered room, " you have plenty of work to do, just darn these stockings will you, while I collect your hats " .

Beatrice threaded her needle and once she was seated in the big arm-chair, her busy tongue began to go.

" What time do you suppose I shall arrive at Paris mother " ? was the first question.

Chapter IV

"Let me see, the boat starts from Newhaven at 11 in the morning," said Mrs.
Langton slowly, "I think you get to Paris
about ten in the evening, though I wont be
sure."

"How nice "! said Beatrice, "is the Vindsor's house very grand "?

"I believe so " replied her mother "at least
they keep fifty servants and nearly everything
is either gold or silver " !

"Gracious " ! exclaimed Beatrice.

"Yes ", said Mrs. Langton, "now Beatrice
bring that darning downstairs, we must finish
packing tomorrow, I will mend that skirt for
you ", and so saying Mrs. Langton left the
room.

CHAPTER V

AT last the eventful day came and found
Beatrice up at six o'clock, putting the last
articles in her bag. By eight o'clock she was
at the station taking the last farewells.

The little ones crowded around her, giving
her chocolate and various sweets to eat on the
way. Mrs. Langton sobbed copiously, and
Mr. Langton as he kissed his daughter pressed
a sovereign into her hand. But at last the

guard waved his flag, the porters slammed the
doors, and Beatrice found herself spinning
away through fields of every shade, fast leaving
Senbury Glen behind and approaching Newhaven Harbour.   Beatrice gave a little sigh
half of joy and half of fear, and then subsided
into her novel and refreshments till the train
stopped and she found herself in the aforesaid
harbour.   There were a great many passengers
going by the Dieppe boat, and Beatrice had some
difficulty to declare her luggage and smuggle
the packet of coffee her thoughtful mother had
put in the sponge bag.   But at last she got on
the boat and once she was seated in her deck
chair gazing on the rough sea, she could
not help shedding a few tears as she thought
of the little brown cottage standing alone on
the outskirts of Senbury Glen.   But she soon
cheered up and asked the stewardess to show
her to her cabin.   The woman obeyed and
walked along the deck till she came to a
battered looking door, which she opened saying—" Here is your cabin miss, your berth is
number 10, and you will find some water to
wash in ".

Beatrice thanked her and entered the room.
A woman five children and a nurse were
seated round the room.   The nurse had two
small babies on her knee which she was trying
to hush to sleep in vain.   The mother was
attempting to comb the hair of a very frantic

little boy and scolding two girls who would
insist on unfastening all the trunks and scatter-
ing the contents on the floor. Beatrice took
no notice of the noisy party, but went to her
corner of the cabin and did her hair and washed
her face in some hard salt water. The
stewardess then brought her some tea and a
bit of cake and Beatrice took the opportunity
to ask her if she was to share the same cabin as
the children and their elders.

"Well," whispered the stewardess, " I am
sorry to say you must, but I expect they will
go on deck soon and then you will be alright
miss ".

Beatrice smiled and tried to read her book
amidst the deafening roars of the babies. But
in a little while the nurse marched them all up
on deck, and the mother soon followed with one
fat baby and a basket of refreshments in her
arms. Then there was peace and Beatrice
quite enjoyed her little dinner of ham sand-
wiches and a cold custard. But about 2
o'clock she began to feel drowsy and enjoyed
a pleasant sleep, and at the end of half an hour
was surprised to find she was in Dieppe.

She gathered her luggage together and a
good natured sailor helped her off the steamer.
She again declared her luggage and went to the
station where she awaited the arrival of the train
to Paris. At last it came up, and Beatrice
found a comfortable carriage well padded with

cushions and rugs, and a fat sulky looking girl in one corner who was busily engaged sucking lemons and studying Bradshaw.

CHAPTER VI

IT was close on ten when the train stopped at Paris, and Beatrice and the fat girl alighted to the platform.

"Do you reside here"? asked the girl in broken English.

"I am here on a visit", replied Beatrice.

"I see ; is it not cold mademoiselle"? said this friendly girl.

"Very", answered Beatrice bottoning the collar of her coat.

"Yes very", continued the girl, "ah Mademoiselle you have no wraps ; take my shawl", and without another word the girl pulled off her shawl and flung it round the shoulders of the astonished Beatrice, and then disappeared into the refreshment room from which she did not reappear again in a hurry. Beatrice was too astonished to speak and hardly liked the coarse woollen shawl which had been so hospitably flung on to her shoulders.

Just as she had with some difficulty found her luggage a very grand footman dressed in

44

green plush came up, and touching his hat said
" Pour le Chateau " ?

Beatrice said " Oui " in a very vague manner,
and soon found herself rumbling along the
streets of Paris in a very comfortable carriage
with her luggage piled round her in a kind of
pyramid and the friendly girl's shawl still
clinging to her shoulders.

Soon the vehicle reduced speed and all at
once Beatrice found herself at the great entrance
porch of " Le Chateau " !

The footman rang the bell and then went
away leaving Beatrice in a transport of fear and
joy on the steps. Soon the door was opened
by a very fat butler with powdered hair and a
green plush uniform.

"What can I do for you " ? he asked with
the air of a king.

" Oh please I have come to stay " said
Beatrice nervously.

" Step inside ", said the courtly butler.

Beatrice did as she was bid and found herself in a most magnificent hall hung with rich
velvet curtains and paved with Turkish carpets,
and supported by gold and silver pillars.

" What name " ? enquired the butler.

Miss Langton ". said Beatrice.

The butler then led her along costly corri-
doors and majestic looking passages and at last
stopped at a door which he flung open and
called in a powerful voice " Miss Langton " !

45

A murmer arose at this announcement and in less than a minute Beatrice was in Mrs. Vindsor's arms being hugged to death almost. " My dear Beatrice " ! she gasped when her kisses were exhausted " how pleased I am to see you ! the steak has just gone down to be kept hot, come and see Clara ".

These comforting words soothed Beatrice, and then Clara came forward to greet her friend.

Clara was a slight thin girl about 19 with very fair hair and blue eyes, she wore a blue satin dress trimmed with real Brussels lace in keeping with Le Chateau, and a spray of blue flowers in her hair.

" My sisters will be down in one minute " she said kindly " their maids are doing their hairs ".

" Oh I see," said Beatrice rapidly taking off her gloves and displaying with some pride her white smooth hands.

" I suppose you are very tired ", said Mrs. Vindsor giving the fire a poke with the toe of her shoe.

" Yes I am," said Beatrice " it was very rough crossing ".

Just then the door opened and two girls entered about 22 and 24 in age. The eldest was by no means beautiful, but she was intensely good. She had small black eyes, and black hair which she wore in a most

46

peculiar manner, it was cut in a fringe in front and gathered into a huge knob behind all except one piece which hung down her back and on the end of which a single red rose was attatched. She was attired in yellow silk and was by no means courteous to Beatrice, her name was Honoria.

The other girl was the most beautiful of the three. She had lovely brown hair and soft blue eyes fringed by sweet long lashes. Her nose and mouth were enough to attract an artist towards her; she was dressed in a lovely pink silk dress and her knob was arrayed by a pink feather. Her name was Margaret and she was known through all Paris as the "sweet young lady with the pathetic blue eyes"! and on the 20th of August (her birthday) not a single person omitted to give her a present. Beatrice thought her lovely and kissed her on both cheeks with hearty good cheer.

And so ended Beatrice first night at Le Chateau.

CHAPTER VII

THE next morning Beatrice had a slight headache and did not rise till the breakfast gong sounded through the walls of the great castle.

Just as she was ready her bedroom was opened and Margaret appeared.

"Oh Beatrice" she cried "isn't it a lovely morning? Mama has just had a note asking us all to Mrs. Middle's garden party this afternoon, there will be a lot of English people there just arrived like yourself".

"Yes very nice", said Beatrice and the two went down to breakfast together.

Mrs. Vindsor and Honoria were already seated at the table enjoying the fragrant meal, but Clara had not yet come down.

"How late you are Margaret" protested Mrs. Vindsor.

"I am sorry Mother" said Margaret cracking her egg.

"So I should hope" said Honoria shaking her head so that the rose at the end of her tail swayed to and fro also.

After the meal was over Clara proposed to take Beatrice for a walk in the gay town as Margaret was going to trim a hat for Mrs. Middle's garden party, and Honoria always did the housekeeping.

Beatrice was delighted at the offer and soon joined Clara in the spacious hall.

"We must go this way" said Clara "as I have to go the Bank for mother".

"Oh alright" said Beatrice taking Clara's arm.

Then followed a little conversation about

nothing in particular, and by the time they reached the Bank Beatrice had quite decided that though Clara was very pleasant and cheery she was not as nice as Margaret who was kindness itself to the strange English girl.

" Would you like to walk up and down while I go into the Bank " ? asked Clara.

" Yes please ", said Beatrice who by no means appreciated Banks, and so saying she left Clara in the office and walked along the gay street. She seemed very strange as she walked through the strange streets and was so taken with the fancy shops that she forgot all about Clara in the bank.

" Dear me ! what lovely gloves " she said as she stopped outside a large drapers shop " we dont have such things in England " !

Just then somebody passed behind her and in so doing brushed against her dress. Beatrice at once looked round and there walking quietly in front as though nothing had happened was a man !

Beatrice looked in amazement at the gentleman calmly receding up the road, and as she looked the form seemed to grow familiar in front of her eyes. Surely she had seen that navy blue suit before, that brown hat and those boots ! Yes ! the very walk was familiar to her. She knew that black curly hair and that well formed back again !—it was Lawrence Cathcart !

Beatrice gave a low cry and covered her face with her hands.

The man looked round and his eyes fell upon the figure of the unhappy Beatrice. He evidently recognized her for with a little hesitation he advanced towards her and taking her arm said not unkindly—" Come with me ".

" I cant," groaned Beatrice.

"You must ", said Lawrence.

Beatrice could do no more but slowly and sadly she followed her enemy.

Many thoughts flashed through her mind during that walk, thoughts that Beatrice will never forget.

At last Lawrence stopped at an Inn door and he mounted the steps and walked in. Beatrice followed in silence.

Presently Lawrence opened a door and the two went into a small but pretty bedroom.

"Now," said Lawrence, turning the key in the door and looking kindly at Beatrice, " have you changed your mind since we last met " ?

The tears welled into Beatrice's blue eyes and rolled down her now death-like cheeks. "Lawrence " she sobbed at length " I wish I could say I had, I almost love you Lawrence but I cannot marry you."

"Very well " answered Lawrence drawing his lips tightly together, " I see my journey to France has been made in vain ; I may add," he continued "that I came here purposely to

encounter you but all in vain ! You have no
real reason for not wishing to become my wife
—it is not possible ; but I will now flee from
you and perhaps when I am laid upon my bed
for the last time and Death has siezed me in
its jaws you will repent of your past wrongs " !

" Oh Lawrence " ! Beatrice almost screamed
in her agony, " just one word before you go " !

" Not one ", replied Lawrence, and with
these words upon his lips he left the unhappy
Beatrice in a swoon upon his floor.

Beatrice had given one hoarse scream as she
fell to the floor, and it brought a couple of
waiters to the room.

" What is it " ? asked one.

" A young lady has fainted " said the other
" run for the doctor quick."

The next instant there was a regular crowd
round Beatrice all intensly interested, and in
less time than it takes to tell old Doctor Holden
was bending over Beatrice's white rigid face.

" She has had some shock I fear " said he
feeling the thin white hand, " can anyone in
the crowd tell me where this lady lives " ?

There was no sound of a reply for the first
few seconds and then came a faint " yes " from
the back of the throng.

" Come forward " cried the doctor. A
rustling and a murmuring of voices ensued, and
then the figure of a young girl rushed forward.
It was Margaret Vindsor who had come out in

search of Clara, and fearing her to be lost had set out to find her.

"Now" said Dr. Holden giving Margaret a chair, "are you any relation to this young lady, and where does she live"?

"Oh Dr. Holden"! cried Margaret "she is a friend of ours and is on a visit to us—oh what shall I do! oh poor Beatrice"!!

"Why Miss Vindsor is it you"? asked Dr. Holden in surprise. "Waiter run for a cab, we must take these ladies back to Le Chateau".

It was not long before the cab stopped at the Inn door and Dr Holden assisted by two waiters, lifted Beatrice into the cab and laid her gingerly on the seat, while Margaret speedily followed, and then the doctor himself jumped in and the downcast party drove back to Le Chateau.

CHAPTER VIII

Mrs. VINDSOR together with Honoria and Clara were waiting breathlessly in the hall when the cab drove up. Honoria flew to the door and the minute she caught sight of the unconscious Beatrice and her sister's pale face she gave a loud scream and tore rapidly to her bedroom. Beatrice was carried to her bedroom at once and the doctor soon left after leaving his directions.

Margaret was in a great state of anxiety, but possessing more self control than the rest of the family she was appointed nurse. Beatrice with the aid of salts and mustard plasters soon came to herself, but Lawrence Cathcart had done his work—rheumatic fever set in and for many days Beatrice hung between life and death. Mr and Mrs Langton were sent for and duly arrived but to no one would Beatrice confide the mystery of her illness. The more she thought of it the more ill she became and Honoria prayed a good deal. By the time she was able to get up her mind was made up. She would look for Lawrence Cathcart, ask his pardon and become his wife. Life offered naught else.

CHAPTER IX

TEN years have passed since the events recorded in my last chapter took place, and Beatrice now a woman of 28, is fair and blooming as ever but with an anxious care-worn expression round her face. She no longer lives in the pretty cottage in Senbury Glen for Mr Langton has lost a great deal of money farming, and he and his family have changed their quarters and live in a dingy little house in a London back street. It would take too long to relate all that has happened on the last years, so I will describe the events as briefly as possible. To begin with little Tina who was always a delicate child has died within the last four years and rests in the churchyard at Senbury Glen. Mary and Lily have had to leave school early and Mary, a girl of twenty is taking lessons in painting, while Lily stays at home.

One thing I must not omit to mention is that Beatrice is still on the look out for Lawrence Cathcart but fears she will never find him.

One Spring morning Beatrice comes down to breakfast and finds Mrs Langton busy with some papers.

"Well mother" she says sadly for her merry tone has completely deserted her, "have you heard of anything I can do to earn my living"?

"yes dear, I think so" replies Mrs Langton glancing nervously at the manuscript in her hand, "you were always fond of nursing were you not Beatrice"?

"yes mother ever since I had that illness" answers Beatrice "it was poor Margaret Vindsor who put the idea in my head".

"Poor Margaret" says Mrs Langton, for Margaret may be numbered among the dead.

"Well Mother what about me"? asks Beatrice presently.

54

Chapter IX

"Oh I was forgetting" answers Mrs Langton "I have heard from Captain Harsh and he says if I care to let you go to India he has a capital place for you as a military hospital nurse".

"To attend to the soldiers wounded in battle"? asks Beatrice.

"Yes dear" replies Mrs Langton, "I will read you the letter—"Madam, ! Hearing of your daughter's wish to become a hospital nurse, I beg to offer my services. If you do not object to soldiers I have a lovely place out here in India where her only work will be to attend to the soldiers in their bungalows either in the night or day as her turn come round. She will live with other nurses in a comfortable house not far from the battle field. She will be expected to bring her own clothes, cups, plates and knives etc : She must be cheerful and kind and must make herself obliging to the soldiers. I will expect her by the next mail.

Believe me, Madam
Yours very sincerely,
George Harsh (Captain of the 109th Regiment)

"That sounds very nice Mother" answers Beatrice "I think I will go".

"What about the character you are expected to have"? says Mrs Langton artfully.

"I think I am both cheerful and kind" says

55

Beatrice hotly "and as to being obliging to the soldiers, anybody could be that".

"Perhaps so," smiles Mrs Langton, "then I will write to Captain Harsh and say you will go by the next mail".

For many days after this Beatrice is busy preparing for the voyage. And at last the eventful day arrives and Beatrice clad for the first time in her nurse's costume steps on board the Victory which is to take her to the wonderful city of Calcutta.

Poor Mr Langton gets quite frantic as he waves his red pocket handkerchief wildly to his beloved daughter for the last time, and Mrs Langton faints on the pier and has to be carried away, which sets the helpless Beatrice sobbing as though her heart would break and she shouts messages till she is hoarse and then sheds many tears which continue on and off till she reaches Calcutta, when the sight of two pleasant nurses dressed like herself, quite cheers her up.

She advances bashfully towards them and says in meek submissive tones "if you please are you military hospital nurses"?

"We are", replies the tallest of the two "our names are Nurse Elsie and Nurse Brandon; of course there is no need to say I am Nurse Brandon."

"Of course not" says Beatrice.

"And you are Nurse Mildred I presume"

asks Nurse Brandon, gently nudging Nurse
Elsie to join in the conversation.

" No my name is Beatrice Langton " replies
Beatrice.

" I know " says Nurse Brandon, " but you
will be known as Nurse Mildred in the wards."

" Oh I see " answer Beatrice glancing at
Nurse Elsie whom she thinks she will like
better than the former.

" And now " says Nurse Brandon " we will
take you to the Residency ; Nurse Elsie kindly
lead the way."

The nurse does as she is told and the three
walk on together. At last they reach a large
building of yellow brick with a placcard on
the door on which is engraved "Nurses'
Residence." Nurse Elsie opens the door and
leads the way to a large airy room in which
some dozen nurses are having tea.

" This is Nurse Mildred ", announces Nurse
Brandon in loud tones, and then seating herself
at the table she continues " Nurse Mildred you
will sit next Nurse Helen tonight ".

Beatrice gazes vaguely round the room
wondering which is Nurse Helen, when suddenly a pretty nurse with chestnut hair and
blue eyes jumps up and announces that she is
Nurse Helen and takes Beatrice to her place.
The tea is good and there is plenty of it, and
together with thick bread and butter and coffee
if preferred to tea, Beatrice thinks it is not a

bad meal. After tea Nurse Brandon shows Beatrice to her room and tells her she need not begin work till to-morrow.

CHAPTER X

THE time speeds rapidly on and Beatrice is now counted as quite an old nurse. She finds her work in the bungalows very pleasant and the soldiers find her most obliging. She works hard and is never tempted to grumble.

One day just as she is settling down to write after tea, after a hard days work, Nurse Helen looks in at the door. "Nurse Mildred", she exclaims "you are to go at once to Bungalow number 5; a wounded soldier has just been taken there and is very ill I fear.

Beatrice jumps up and putting on her bonnet walks quickly to the 5th bungalow. It is a little white one on the outskirts of the jungle and close to the battle field, and in it there is a bed, two chairs, a jug, basin and table. Beatrice takes hold of a small cup and measures some ointment into it, and then taking a sponge bathes the man's wounds. He is a very thin man with long slender hands and black hair and eyes, and at a first glance Beatrice sees that he is on the point of death. She does all she can for him and then at his wish reads some Holy Scriptures to him. Then seeing his eyes droop she goes to the other end of the bungalow and waits.

Presently she hears a weak voice say "Beatrice"!

She starts, it is a long time since that name has fallen on her ears.

"Beatrice, dont you know me"? says the voice once more.

In a minute Beatrice is at his side clasping his hand in hers. "Oh Lawrence, Lawrence"! she cries.

Then there is silence.

"Lawrence can you ever forgive me"? moans Beatrice at last.

"Forgive you my darling? it is the one thing I have lived for" says Lawrence.

"Accept me as your lawful wife," cries Beatrice bending over him.

"Yes darling, yes," says Lawrence faintly. He then tells her in a few words how in despair he had given up everything and gone into the Army and lived only long enough to forgive Beatrice, for that day he had received his death wound in a sharp battle with the enemy.

"And now," he adds, "I shall die happy, and will you remember in after years (for I shall not live to) how here it was our hearts were re-united—once more joined together, here it was I accepted you for my wife, and here it is therefore that Love lies Deepest"!

"Oh my dear"! groans Beatrice heavily, "Lawrence, here is what I was going to have given you at the French Inn," and she presses a pair of golden links into his dying hand.

He smiles back at her and says "keep them darling as a remembrance of me."

Beatrice's only answer is a wild kiss, the last Lawrence will ever receive, the memory of which follows him to Eternity, the next minute he falls back with a groan.

Beatrice stands for a rigid moment and then falls prone beside the bed.

And there is only one in all this wide world who knows for certain if Lawrence Cathcart died a happy death.

The Hangman's Daughter

PART I

CHAPTER I

PROLOGUE

JOHN WINSTON had entered into manhood with every prospect of a bright and brilliant future.

His parents had died leaving him a nice little legacy and a great deal of land for farming But with all this good fortune, things did not seem to go right with him.

To begin with, he was idle and did not care for farming, so he let land waste away till it was good for nothing, and he was forced to sell it. He then encountered a severe loss of money, and by degrees sank lower and lower in the world till he at last found himself a penniless man with barely enough to keep a roof over his head.

His only resourse then was marriage. There were plenty of rich girls about whose parents would be glad to find a suitable husband for them. John Winston was suitable enough, for he was good looking, witty, and had a certain amount of good sense ; but his kind heart would not allow him to fall in love with these girls merely on account of their riches, so had to look out for someone he really loved.

63

During these explorations he met Helen Carline, a young girl, poor, and with no relations in the world. She was wondrously pretty, with a profusion of fluffy golden hair and sad blue eyes, which spoke all their thoughts.

Of course John Winston fell in love with her at once and proposed accordingly. After a little hesitation she accepted and John Winston's joy was beautiful to witness.

The married couple took a little cottage on the outskirts of the Malvern Hills, and engaged one servent Jane Marshland, by name, about whom we shall hear more later on.

In the spring of the following year a little girl was born as a crowning joy to the young husband and wife.

But three months afterwards Mrs. Winston died of fever, which she caught when visiting a gipsy encampment near her home. So at an early age, little Helen (for that was the child's name) was left without a mother, but she lacked no love or tenderness, for Mr. Winston's only care was for his beloved child, and Jane Marshland now the nurse, did every thing she could for the child's health and comfort.

Mr. Winston had to give up his dear little home, and retire with Jane and his baby to lodgings in London till he heard of some employment.

At last he found something not very satisfactory, but as nothing else offered, he decided to take it. It was to perform the office of hangman in a small country town in Hants, by the name of Kenalham.

It was not a nice position to be in certainly, and Mr. Winston's nerves were not strong, but the payment was good, and after all only about two people were hung a year at Kenalham.

So with a sinking heart Mr. Winston packed up his goods and departed with his child and servant to the little cottage in Kenalham, already furnished for him. It was a nice little house, and Mr. Winston smiled as he entered the drawing room, "after all" he said to Jane, "so few people are hung here that nearly all my time will be devoted to my darling Helen," and he kissed the rosy face of the child.

So, now having explained the position of my story I will skip over a few years and go on again at the time when Helen had grown up into a charming sweet mannered girl.

CHAPTER II

THE COTTAGE BY THE HILL

THE little village of Kenalham was situated in the south of Hants and lay at the bottom of some picturesquely grouped hills.

No river watered the little town, but a broad

stream wound through the neighbouring
medows giving a rich green shade to the grass
on its banks ; the high green hills stood out
clear and tall against the blue sky, and the
ruins of an old castle on the top of one of the
heights gave a strange weird appearance. To
add to the strangeness of this little scene, at the
bottom of the very hill on which the ruins
stood was a villa of the modern kind nestling
amidst a woody dell of beach trees. This was
no other than the residence of Mr. John Winston and his daughter Helen, and it went by
the name of " Beach Dale."

It was a charming little house and had the
preveleage of possessing a beautiful view both
back and front. The front looked out across
miles of woodland scenery with no sign of
human inhabetance any where safe a single
cottage which stood out like a white speck
among the greenness which surrounded it.

The back looked out on the lovely blue hills,
and far away in the distant loomed the white
cliffs of Portsmouth.

Having now given the reader a correct idea
of the surroundings of " Beach Dale " I will
endevour to described Helen Winston.

At the time my story opens, our heroine was
a charming young lady of nineteen years. She
had an abundance of dark brown, almost black
hair, curling gracefully over her forehead. Her
beautiful brown eyes were headed by well

marked eye brows of a lovely black ; her complexion was like that of a blush rose and her
pretty little nose and mouth added to the charm
of her features.

Here character I will leave to be found out
and only say that she was passionately fond of
her father and devoted all her life solely to him.

Trouble and care had made Mr. Winston
look old before his time. He was only 54,
yet his hair and beard were completely
grey. He had a kind quiet face and blue eyes,
he had a rather wide mouth with a nervous
twitch at each corner. He fully returned his
daughter's love and considering he had taught
her entirely himself she was comparatively
cleaver girl.

CHAPTER III

THE SECRET SAFE

DURING all the years Mr. Winston had lived
in Kenalham he had only made one friend a
Mr. Cyril Sheen. He was thirty years of age
and a bachelor. He too had no friends in the
village but Mr. Winston, so he was constantly
at " Beach Dale." He was very fond of Helen
and had often attempted to make love to her,
but she was so completely innocent of his
intentions that he felt quite bashful and dare
not begin.

One morning, early in May, Mr. Winston and his daughter were just finishing their breakfast when Marshland came in with a letter which she handed to her master.

"A letter?" said Mr. Winston opening his eyes, "who can it be from?"

"Business, father I'm sure" replied Helen with a smile.

"I think not," said Mr. Winston wisely and he proceeded to tear open the envelope and persue its contents.

As he read the letter his face became first thoughtful, then puzzled and then it broke into a smile and lastly Mr. Winston burst into a fit of laughter and took a sip of his untasted tea. He then turned to his daughter for the first time.

"Do you know who this is from, Helen?" he said.

"No father I don't" answered Helen.

"Perhaps it will need a little explanation" replied Mr. Winston. "You have heard me speak of your cousins the Lincarrols haven't you?"

"Oh yes I know" said Helen "they are very rich aren't they?"

"Yes" said Mr. Winston slowly, "very."

"Well father what about them?" said Helen.

"Did I ever mention Gladys to you," enquired Mr. Winston.

68

"Oh yes" said Helen, "she is the pretty one isn't she?"

"Yes she is quite the "flower of the flock" I belive" replied Mr. Winston; "the others are decidedly plain."

"Well what about Gladys?" enquired Helen.

"Well she is going to be married shortly, and so she proposes coming here next week for a little while and bring her future husband with her. What do you say to that?" asked Mr. Winston.

Helen's pretty face was beaming with novelty and pleasure.

"How lovely father" she gasped; I do hope she will be nice."

"What about a bedroom for her?" said Mr. Winston.

"Oh! there's the little attic in the loft" replied Helen. "I'm sure that is good enough."

"What about the furniture for it? at present it is completely bare and full of cobwebs," said Winston.

"I forgot about that," said Helen. "Well she can Have the best bedroom."

"Yes" said Mr. Winston "but where is the young man to go?"

"What young man?" said Helen.

"James Palsey" said Mr. Winston referring to the letter in his hand.

Helen's face fell and her eyes filled with

69

tears. " I'm afraid father " she said " we shall
have to refuse them, for if the attic has to be
used I certainly have no money to furnish it
with and I know you have not."

"Don't make too sure my lass " said her
father, " wait a little."

He got up as he spoke and taking a small
key from his pocket went towards the left
hand corner of the mantlepiece.

" Come closer Helen, come closer," he said
keeping his eyes on his daughter.

Helen followed her father closely, her eyes
with a startled expression in them and her lips
quivering with emotion. Mr. Winston lifted
a portion of the red velvit curtain which
screaned the fire place, and then to Helen said :

"Do you notice anything peculiar about this
part of the wall, my child."

"No father, except that there is a little hole
·ust in the middle," replied Helen.

"Ah ! you notice that ? " said Mr. Winston.

"Yes " said Helen under her breath.

"Now watch me " said Mr. Winston.

Helen needed no second bidding ; her eyes
seemed rivited to the little hole.

Mr. Winston placed the key into the hole
and turned it twice round. Immeadiately a
little spring door flew open displaying two
well constructed shelves of solid oak.

" This is my secret safe," said Mr. Winston,
" known to no one but myself."

"Father!" cried Helen catching hold of his arm.

"Don't get excited, Helen" said her father. "I am going to disclose all the secrets of this safe to you. Do you perceive that the top shelf is faced in by a thin wire gauze with a handle to the left hand side?"

"Yes father" replied Helen.

"Well, nobody can get at the contents of that shelf without my knowing it."

"Why father?" asked Helen.

"Because there are two ways of opening it. Try to open it yourself and then I will explain it to you" said Mr. Winston.

Helen with nervous fingers took hold of the handle and turned it; the gauze door flew open and at the same time a bell began to ring loud and furiously.

Helen drew back in amazement.

"Cant Marshland hear it? Why doesn't she come up" asked Helen.

"She would not trouble to come up for she knows my secret" said Mr. Winston.

"Oh! I see" said Helen.

"Well to procead" said Mr. Winston. "If Marshland or I heard that bell we should know the safe was being robbed and come up at once."

"Of course" said Helen.

"But there is another way of opening the safe known only to me" said Mr. Winston closing the gauze door; try any way you like to open that door I don't think you will find the right way."

Helen pushed and banged at the door trying every way, but in vain, the door would not move.

"Now I will show the right way," said Mr. Winston,

As he spoke he placed his thumb on a brass nail and the gauze door rose, instead of opening, and without any noise displayed the contents of the secret safe.

"How wonderfull" said Helen.

"Would you like to see the contents?" said Mr. Winston.

"Oh! yes father" replied Helen.

Mr. Winston put his hand on the shelf and brought out a leather bag.

"It is full of gold" he said weighing it in his hand, "the savings of a life time".

"Oh father" gasped Helen.

Mr. Winston took out 10 gold peices and the rest he left in the bag "this will pay for the furnishing of the attic" he said.

"So it will" said Helen brightly.

Mr. Winston put the bag back and took out a little ivory box and displayed some magnificent jewilery to his daughter's dazzled eyes, "this was all all left to you by your mother's will," he said.

"Really!" said Helen, "I can't belive it."

The jewils consisted of two broachs, one set entirely in diamonds, the other a horseshow set in rubies ; a gold watch, chain and seals ; a nexlet of pearls and a gold bracelet fastenned with a ruby heart.

Mr. Winston placed the bracelet on Helen's slender arm ; "this" he said "was to be given you in your nineteenth year, the other jewils by your mother's will will be given to you when you come of age.

"How lovely" cried Helen glancing at the circlet of gold on her wrist.

"I will now lock up the rest of the things" said Mr. Winston "and mind Helen, not a word of this is ever to be revealed."

"Never father" said Helen kissing him.

Mr. Winston had barely shut the safe and closed the curtain when the door opened and in came Cyril Sheene.

"Good morning Winston" he cried hastily, "I thought I'd just pop in and see if Helen would come out with me."

"Why Cyril we didn't expect you half so early" said Helen blushing.

"No I'm sure you did'nt replied Cyril, "but you will come out wont you ?"

"Oh certainly" said Helen and she ran up to get her hat.

CHAPTER IV

THE PROPOSAL

CYRIL SHEENE, as I have already said was thirty years of age and a bachelor.

He was short and fat and had fair sleek hair parted in the middle, mild blue eyes and a silly sort of expression all over his face.

In ten minutes Helen came down again in a neatly fitting grey jacket and a large straw hat with a few scarlet poppies trailing over the brim. She looked very pretty and Cyril's face shone with pleasure as he regarded her.

" Wont you come out father " ? asked Helen, " I suppose we are going on the hills are'nt we Cyril " ?

I thought we might go and sit by the old castle, it is such a glorious day " responded Cyril.

" Do come father " said Helen.

" I don't think I can " said Mr. Winston " I must go to the town this morning "

" Very well " said Helen ; and then while Cyril Sheene was looking for his stick, she seized an opportunity to ask her father " shall I tell Cyril about Gladys coming ? " " Yes " replied Mr. Winston " but mind not a word about the safe." "Oh no " answered Helen, and then with a lively little jump she ran after Cyril who was already walking down the garden path.

It was a perfect morning, the sun shone brightly, lighting up all the scenery around; the birds were singing in the beach trees close by and the rippling of the little stream was as sweet music to the ear.

"Do you know Helen, I had an engagement in London today, but I put it off to come out with you" said Cyril, as they commenced to climb the hill.

"Oh indeed!" replied Helen "that was very kind of you."

"Oh no" answered Cyril "I would far rather be out here than in London."

"I quite agree with you there" said Helen "it would be horrid to be in smoky London today."

"Yes" said Cyril "especially without you."

"Oh rubbish" laughed Helen and she stopped down to pick a buttercup.

"Indeed it is not rubbish" replied Cyril "when a man loves, he finds it hard to be away from the object of his love."

"Oh does he?" said Helen "but then I am not the object of your love."

"Yes you are Helen," said Cyril, making an attempt to squeaze her hand."

"My dear boy" said Helen, "I do wish you would not talk such nonsense."

"Excuse me" answered Cyril, getting rather red "I am a man.

"Are you really?" said Helen carelessly.

"Now look here Helen, don't be aggrivating " said the lover " you know quite well I love you and why I have come here."

They had reached the castle now and sat down by the ruined walls.

" Why have I come up here ? " asked Cyril again.

" I suppose because it is more breezy than the town " replied Helen.

" Don't be silly Helen " said Cyril pulling up a tuft of grass.

" I am not the least silly " said Helen smiling beneath her handkerchief.

" No of course you're not darling " cried Cyril putting his arm round her waist.

" You must'nt call me " darling " Cyril " replied the girl shyly.

" Yes I must " said Cyril getting a little closer.

" Oh well for once in a way perhaps it does'nt matter " said Helen.

" Well the long and the short of it is Helen " said Cyril " I want to marry you ?

" Really " said Helen " you've been long enough getting to the point."

" Have I ? " said Cyril shyly " well now that I have come to it, do you love me enough to marry me ? "

" Ye-s " replied Helen slowly.

" You seem rather doubtful " said Cyril.

" It's best to be so at first " replied Helen.

" Not in my case surely " answered Cyril, "oh Helen do say yes and make me a happy man."

" Yes " murmured Helen softly.

" Oh you angel " gasped Cyril " do you really mean it ? "

" Of course I do " said Helen, " and I *do* love you Cyril."

" Thank you so much " said Cyril " well now let's hurry home and ask your father I'm in such a terrific hurry."

" Don't be absurd " said Helen " I want to stay in the sunshine."

" Anything to please you dear " said Cyril re-seating himself on the grass.

" Cyril, I think you'll make a model husband " said Helen.

" I'm sure I will " laughed Cyril and with that they got up to walk home.

At the bottom of the hill they spied Mr. Winston. He looked up as he saw them coming and waved his hand furiously.

When they met Mr. Winston he turned directly to Helen, " what do you think Helen, I've furnished the attic all by myself, the only thing Marshland did was to scrub the floor and nail up the curtains."

" How nice " said Helen " but father I've something far more important to tell you."

" Dont say it my child " said the old man " your faces tell me what it is and I give my consent on the spot."

And he plunged his stick into the ground to mark the vehemence of his words.

CHAPTER V

GLADYS LINCARROL

THE week that followed that day was a happy one indeed. Helen and Cyril were more together than ever and then too each day brought it nearer to when Gladys was to come.

At last Monday morning came, and Helen was so excited she could hardly eat her dinner, and Mr. Winston got quite cross when she refused some beautiful cherry pie.

"Do hurry up father" exclaimed Helen at last, "I want to have the room nice and tidy for Gladys and Mr. Palsey."

"My dear I wont starve for any amount of grand ladies" replied Mr. Winston heartily.

Helen smiled languidly and began to arrange the flower stand by the window.

At 4 o'clock precisely a dainty little dog cart drew up at Beach Dale. Helen, peeping from behind the drawing room curtains, saw, first a tall man dressed in a blue suit and black hat and gloves, jump down from the cart and hold out his hand to a young lady who tripped lightly down and tossed a silver coin to the coachman.

The next moment the drawing room door was flung open and Marshland's clear voice was heard announcing, "Miss Lincarrol—Mr. Palsey."

78

"Oh dear Gladys, I am so delighted to see you" cried Helen in her sweetest tones.

"And I am equally glad to meet you" cried Gladys, "and allow me to introduce my future husband James Palsey."

"How do you do" said Mr. Palsey gravely as he held out his well gloved hand.

At that minute Mr. Winston entered the room dressed in his best things.

"Well Gladys my dear and how are you he cried cheerfully "what a big person you are to be sure, quite half a head taller than Helen I declare."

Gladys laughed affectedly and held out her small hand ; she then introduced Mr. Palsey, who, during all this merriment had stood as grave as a judge.

"Do come and have some food pleaded Helen pointing to the dainty little tea equipage already set out on a bamboo table by the open window.

"Oh thank you" said Gladys and she began to take off her gloves and turn up her veil preparatory to eating.

"Wont you take a seat Mr. Palsey?" asked Helen as she poured out the tea.

"Thanks" replied the gentleman and he sat down on the edge of a whicker chair. Here will be a good oppertunity to describe Gladys Lincarrol and her young man.

Mr. Palsey was a tall broad shouldered man

about 37, with a solemn face and large hands. His black hair was curly and plentiful and his small green eyes twinkled queerly if he was at all pleased. He was attired in blue, as I said before and in addition to this he wore patent leather boats and a crimson tie.

Gladys was also tall, but very slim. She had golden hair with a reddish tinge and blue eyes. She was very pale and her mouth had a peculiar twitch of conciet. She wore a lovely pink muslin dress and kid gloves to match. A large white hat adorned her pretty head, and she wore a bunch of violets at her neck.

Tea over, Helen proposed a stroll around the village.

"Oh yes, that will be very nice, don't you think so Jim?" asked Gladys.

"Yes I do, thanks" replied Mr. Palsey.

So the trio linked arms and walked slowly down the garden path, and Mr. Winston settled himself comfortably once more and prepared to read the "Star."

CHAPTER VI

A DISOPPOINTING LETTER

HE had barely got through the first paragraph when Marshland entered with a letter.

"For you sir" she said placing it on her master's lap.

"Thanks" said Mr. Winston opening the envelope as he spoke.

The letter ran thus :

H.M. Prison,
Warwick

Dear Sir,

      You are requested to come up here by the first train tomorrow morning to hang Mr. Smith, who has lately murdered his wife and three children. It is a serious case, and I am sure you will sympathize.

Belive me dear sir
Yours etc
C. L. Porter (head warder of the
county prison).

To J. Winston Esq : Beach Dale, Kenalham Hants.

Mr. Winston sighed as he closed the letter.

"Oh dear oh dear" he cried, "here I have to leave my happy home, just when Gladys and James have arrived, Marshland" he added.

"Yes sir" said the servant coming forward.

"I shall have to leave home early tomorrow" said Mr. Winston "how will you get on with out me ? "

"Oh sir, I think we shall get on all right" responded Marshland " I'll keep an eye on the young ladies and Mr. Palsey will cheer them up I know."

" I dont know that " said Mr. Winston " he seems a very dull gentleman."

" Do he really sir " said Marshland " well I'm sure I'm very sad."

" But do you think you can mannage without me ?   I shall not be away more than three days " asked Mr. Winston.

"Oh yes sir, dont you fret" replied Marshland and now is there anything I can do for you ? "

" No nothing thank you " said Mr. Winston " but when the young ladies and Mr. Palsey come in, send Miss Helen to me."

" Yes sir " said Marshland quitting the room.

Barely had the door closed on Marshlands comely figure, when it opened again and Cyril Sheene came bounding in.

" Hullo Winston " he cried " I heard you had some friends down, so I thought I'd just drop in and be introduced."

" They're all out at present " said Mr. Winston with a vain attempt at a smile, " sit down wont you they'll be in soon."

Cyril flung himself down in an arm chair and then glanced at Mr. Winston.

" Why Winston old fellow " he cried, you dont look yourself, is anything up ? "

" Oh nothing said Mr. Winston tapping the table nervously."

" Now look here " said Cyril " you cant get round me like that, I know something is wrong, you might as well tell me."

82

" Very well Cyril I'll tell you " said Mr. Winston and he handed the letter to Cyril, who read it carefully through. As he did so a marked change came over his face, a change from a pleasant faced young man to that of a stern, cold, yet pleased person.

" So you're off tomorrow ? " remarked he as he folded the paper.

" Yes I suppose so " said Mr. Winston.

" How you must feel leaving the girls all alone " said Cyril.

" I do " said Mr. Winston, " but I know Marshland will take good care of them and you'll look in wont you ? "

" Well I was about to suggest going up with you " said Cyril " I know a few friends in Warwick and you'll be all the better for a companion."

" It is kind of you Cyril " said Mr. Winston " but I'd rather you stopped to take care of Helen."

" Oh Helen will be all right with Marshland and Mr. Palsey in the house " said Cyril " I think you need me more."

" I suppose I do " replied Mr. Winston " but my poor little Helen."

" Well I'll stay if you like, but you wont be away more than three days and what Helen wants with me hanging about I dont know." said Cyril.

" Well I'll take your advice and accept you

as a companion, and thanks a thousand times Cyril " replied Mr. Winston.

At that moment the door opened and Helen came running in.

" Well father dear " she said, " I was told you wanted me, so I just came down while Gladys changes her dress."

" Yes dear " said Mr. Winston I am afraid I have some rather bad news for you."

" Oh dear father what is it ? " exclaimed Helen kneeling down by the chair.

" I must go to Warwick early to-morrow dear on a hanging matter " replied Mr. Winston " I shall be back in three days."

" Oh father " cried Helen " just when Gladys and Mr. Palsey have come down Oh I am sorry " and her pretty eyes filled with tears.

" Yes dear I am sorry too " remarked Mr. Winston slowly, " but you'll be all right wont you ? "

" Oh yes father " said Helen " I was not thinking of myself, but it always knocks you up so, and just when we're all so happy."

" Well Cyril has offered to go with me and keep me company " said Mr. Winston " you wont miss him much will you ? "

" Oh Cyril I am glad " exclaimed Helen. " I feel far easier now, you'll take such care of father I know."

" Yes Helen I will " said Cyril folding Helen in his arms and kissing her forehead.

"Thank you Cyril" said Helen returning her lover's kiss.

Soon after Gladys and Mr. Palsey came in, and a merry farewell evening was spent, Cyril at the head of the fun.

Next morning Helen was up early toasting some bread for her father's breakfast; she made the table and room as cosy as she could and then waited her fathers coming down.

He came at last looking worn and pale but he enjoyed his meal and cheered up a little as he ate it.

"Now dear, is your portmanteau ready?" enquired Helen trying hard to keep back her tears.

"Yes dear quite" returned the father "and Cyril will meet me at the station you know."

"Yes he told me so" replied Helen.

"Well goodbye darling, keep a good heart and I'll be back on Thursday at the latest" said Mr. Winston.

"Goodbye dear father" rejoined the girl "I'll try and be cheerful but it is hard you know."

"I know it dear" said Mr. Winston and then turning to Marshland he added "goodbye Marshland, take good care of the young ladies and keep an eyes on Mr. Palsey."

"I will sir" returned Marshland and then she and Helen stood at the door the latter waving her handkerchief to the dear father who was never more to enter his happy home in Kenalham.

CHAPTER VII

THE ALARM

HELEN WINSTON found it very hard to be merry without her father, but she did her best and Gladys took her little attentions very kindly.

"What do you propose doing now? she asked when breakfast was cleared away.

"I must attend to the housekeeping first and then I thought a walk on the hills would be nice" answered Helen.

"Very good" said Gladys "we can go and visit the old castle you talk so much about."

"Yes" said Helen, and she tripped down stairs, more for the pleasure of a comforting talk with Marshland than to order the dinner.

In an hour's time they were all ready and started on their breezy walk.

"How lovely it is up here," remarked Gladys.

"Yes is'nt it beautiful" replied Helen thinking of the last time she was up there."

The little promenade quite cheered Helen up, and she and Gladys did some shopping in the afternoon while Mr. Palsey stayed at home to smoke his pipe.

The next day passed pretty much the same as the first and by Thursday morning Helen was all smiles again, knowing that by tea-time her father would be home again.

In the afternoon she went out and bourght a tea cake for tea. She had tea laid out on the best bamboo table with the blue and gold tea cups and she also put fresh flowers in all the vases and all together the little drawing room had a truly home-like aspect.

At 4 o'clock a ring was heard at the front door.

" How funny of father to ring " cried Helen " I thought he would be sure to come in and supprise me."

"Perhaps he thought it would supprise you more if he rung," replied Gladys.

" Ah perhaps so " responded Helen giving a last touch to the pink rose-buds which drooped prettily over the china vases.

At that moment Marshland entered the room with a frightened look on her face.

Coming up she handed a telegram to Helen "its given me such a turn miss " she explained "them telegrams always seem to carry bad news."

Helens face grew pale and she hastily opened the envelope.

The moment her eyes rested on the words, she uttered a cry of anguish and flung the telegram away from her. " Oh I know its father " she cried.

" Hush hush miss " said Marshland soothingly and picking up the telegram she too read
the fatel words.   The telegram ran as follows :

Come at once, a terrible thing has happened.
Sheene.

Marshland's honest face grew ashy as she
read the words, but she tried to control her
feelings for Helens sake.

" Well miss it is a terrible thing " she said
" but we can but hope for the best, what train
will you go by miss."

" Oh I dont know, dont ask me," cried poor
Helen.

" Don't cry so Helen dear " said Gladys
" after all it may not be as bad as Mr. Sheene
thinks."

" Wont you allow me to come to Warwick
with you Miss Winston ? " asked Mr. Palsey
kindly.

" You're very kind " sobbed Helen, " but
Gladys wont like it."

" Dont think of me for one instant " said
Gladys, patting Helen's head " of course you'll
go with her James and Marshland and I will
keep house till you come back."

" I had better go tonight " said Helen
getting up from the sofa and glancing at the
pretty little tea table, which five minutes ago
she had arranged with such love and care.

" Yes miss, the telegram says at once "

replied Marshland, " I wonder when the next
train is."

" I can tell you " cried Mr. Palsey producing
a time table from his pocket and running his
finger down the column.

" Poor Helen " said Gladys kissing her
fondly.

" Seven fifteen is the next " said Mr. Palsey,
" that'll give you nice time to get ready, and it
gets to Warwick at 11-30."

" That will do " replied Helen " will you
put my things together for me, I feel so faint."

" Yes dearie " replied Marshland. " Now
Helen dear you rest on the sofa and I'll bring
you some tea " said Gladys. Helen flung herself down, quite worn out.

Gladys gave her a cup of strong tea and
bathed her hot head with eau de cologne.

" I'll go and order the dog-cart, to drive us
to the station " said Mr. Palsey.

" Yes be quick James, you must not be late "
replied Gladys.

For in an hour's time all was ready. Helen,
with a white shawl over her face was standing
at the door while Mr. Palsey put the bags into
the dog cart.

" Goodbye Helen dear " cried Gladys " keep
up a good heart and James will take every care
of you."

" Goodbye Gladys " said Helen " and thanks
so much for sparing him to me."

"Goodbye Miss Helen my love" cried poor old Marshland wiping her eyes on her apron, "write as soon as you can and let me know how the master is."

"Yes of course I will" cried Helen, jumping into the dog cart, "goodbye all, goodbye" and in an other minute the dog cart was out of sight, and Marshland returned to her work, and Gladys to the deserted drawing room.

CHAPTER VIII

BAD NEWS

THE journey on which Helen and Mr. Palsey had set out was a very long one indeed and, May though it was, the night was very chilly.

Helen shivered as she got into the train and drew her shawl round her. Mr. Palsey had taken first class tickets, and so soothing was the motion of the train and so comfortable the seat in which she found herself that Helen soon dropped asleep.

"Now I can think over things a bit," said Mr. Palsey taking some papers from a black bag by his side, "jolly nice of Gladys to suggest me coming up here, though she didn't know why I wanted to come poor girl; odd that I didn't hear from Sheene today, I quite expected a line or a telegram to say how matters stand.

" It may here be mentioned that Mr. Palsey
and Cyril Sheen were by no means new aquain-
tances and had met many times in London and
even once or twice before at Kenalham.

" Odd how Cyril found out about that secret
shelf mused Mr. Palsey " a whole bag of gold
he said, how Winston saved it I don't know,
ah he was a rich man with all his poor living
and scanty furniture. I think there were some
jewils in the safe too but of course it is the
money, the gold I'm putting myself to this for
and with a cold laugh, he drew out some closely
written papers and read them eagerly, putting
pencil marks by certain paragraphs in the
document.

The train flew on nearing Warwick rapidly.

At last Helen awoke with a start and found
Mr. Palsey taking forty winks opposite her.

She rubbed her eyes and looked out of the
window, " how dark it is " she thought and its
raining too, how horrible and she nestled under
her fluffy shawl. Presently the train stopped
with a jerk and Mr. Palsey woke up.

" This is Warwick " he said picking up his
bag " train's late and it is twenty to twelve.

" How late " quoth Helen and with a sigh
she followed Mr. Palsey on to the crowded
platform.

It was a dreary sight which met the weary
girl's eyes. The rain was pouring heavily and
the whole station looked wet and miserable.

The gas lights flickered in the wind making hideous shadows on the walls. The porters, cold and cross looking, poor things, were bustling about, crying the name of the station at the tops of their voices, and a thin shaggy dog, evidently lost, was howling pitiably, tending by no means to cheer poor Helen's quaking heart.

"I thought Cyril would be sure to meet you" said Mr. Palsey suddenly "you go into the waiting room and warm yourself and I'll walk up the road a bit and see if I see him, for I dont know what house to go to do you?"

"No" said Helen, "oh Mr. Palsey I'm so unhappy and with a faint cry she turned away and buried her face in her shawl.

"Poor thing" thought Mr. Palsey "she cant guess the worst yet," out loud he added "hush Miss Winston, you are over fatigued, that is all, would you like a cup of coffee? the refreshment room is not yet closed."

"I could'nt drink or eat" replied Helen sadly "I'll go and sit by the fire while you look for Cyril."

"Very well" said Mr. Palsey, and he turned round and went off in an opposite direction.

Helen entered the waiting room and sat by the fire her tired eyes covered with her hands. Presently she raised her white face and glanced at the clock. Two old ladies sitting near, noticed her pale frightenned face.

" Have you come a long journey " asked one "you look very tired."

" I am very tired, and miserable too " broke forth Helen in the fullness of her heart " oh why am I dragged up here in this cruel fashion, oh what has happened to father ? " she burst into heart broken sobbing.

The old ladies looked very much alarmed and after bidding Helen a good night, gathered up their wraps and departed.

The time sped on and still neither Cyril nor Mr. Palsey arrived.

Helen grew terrified and was on the point of going out on to the platform when the door opened and the two men appeared.

Mr. Palsey looked much the same, Cyril was clad in a heavy ulster and his face was white and scared.

Cyril was speaking as the two entered and Helen caught the last words, "just as we could have wished " he was saying. " Oh Cyril Cyril " cried Helen and she flung herself into his arms.

" My darling " gasped Cyril and a queer gurgle sounded in his throat. " What is it Cyril, what has happened ? " cried Helen, clutching hold of his coat.

" Hush darling " said Cyril, " come outside.

Helen was quite overcome by now and she allowed herself to be led out by Cyril and Mr. Palsey.

" Shall you tell her tonight " whispered Mr.
Palsey.

" It is better to get it over " replied Cyril,
" Helen dear, be prepared for bad news."

" Yes yes anything " gasped Helen nervously
" father is ill I know very ill, oh Cyril tell me
quickly "

" Worse than that " said Cyril and he clasped
her tightly to him.

" Not dying moaned Helen, " oh Cyril not
dying.

Cyril said nothing, but Mr. Palsey whispered
" out with it Sheene, she must know soon."

" He is dead " cried Helen wildly," say the
words Cyril say them."

Cyril bowed his head " yes " he murmered
" dead—murd——

" Hush " whispered Mr. Palsey striking him
on the arm, " you idiot, keep quiet."

With a shriek, Helen tore herself from
Cyril's grasp and ran like the wind, she herself
knew not wither ; at the station gate her
strength failed her, she turned, she tottered,
she tried to scream and fell insensible at the
feet of the villians.

CHAPTER IX

HELEN'S ACCIDENT

CYRIL and Mr. Palsey lost no time in conveying Helen to a cab which was waiting outside. They placed her on one of the seats and bade the cabman drive directly to number 2 Medina Road, where Cyril was lodging.

"How will you manage about the money Cyril?" presently asked Mr. Palsey.

"Dont speak to me of money?" cried Cyril bitterly, "oh Helen Helen" and he bent over his unconcious sweetheart.

"Pon me word Cyril" cried Mr. Palsey "you're a born idiot, the girl will soon recover, you'll marry her and we'll go halfs with the money, its simply ridiculous the way you mople and mumble over her, let her alone I say and tell me how the murd—the bussiness went off."

"I've told you twice it was very successful" replied Cyril impatiantly.

"You're trying to hide something I can see" cried Mr. Palsey passionately, "you'd best tell me, or not a farthing of the money shall be yours."

"I don't see that" said Cyril cooly, "you dont even know where the safe is." Mr. Palsey bit his lips in suppressed anger. Cyril's words were stiningly true and made him boil with passion. "Here we are" said Cyril, as the cab stopped at a dimly lighted street corner.

"Hi cabman, get down and open the door" screamed Mr. Palsey.

The man shuffled down from the box and opened the door.

"Any luggage" he asked roughly.

"No" replied Mr. Palsey "there is a young lady fainted and we are going to carry her into this house."

"Right" responded the man and he stood aside while Cyril and Mr. Palsey came gingerly out carrying Helen between them.

As they were ascending the steps a rough looking man in a torn red shirt and battered hat came up and addressed himself to Cyril.

"Hi sir" he cried out "what about that £10 you promised; I'm a poor starving man and I can't wait much longer.

"Bother" muttered Cyril "here man will a shilling suffice for this evening, I'll pay the rest tomorrow."

"All right" grumbled the man, "unless you pay up tomorrow it'll be the last job I do for you," and with an oath the man departed.

Cyril led the way into a dimly lighted parlour and with Mr. Palseys help Helen was soon arranged on the sofa.

Some supper consisting of cold mutton, vegitables and a jug of ale was laid out on a round table in the centre of the room, and a small paraffin lamp burnt on the mantelshelf. Going over to this last object Cyril screwed it up, so that its glare fell, full on Helen's face.

"Why she's hurt herself terribly" cried Cyril in alarm, pointing to a wound in her forehead from which blood had been streaming down her face.

"Is your landlady up?" enquired Mr. Palsey seriously.

"I should rather doubt it, why?" asked Cyril.

"Because Miss Winston should be taken to her bedroom at once, I'm afraid its a bad cut" replied Mr. Palsey.

"I'll ring" responded Cyril and he acted accordingly.

In ten minutes or so an oldish woman entered holding a candle and her garments had evidently been flung on in a hurry.

"What now sir?" she asked.

"Sorry for disturbing you Mrs. Pollard but this young lady of mine has had a terrible fall and must be taken to her bedroom at once, we thought it was only a faint said Cyril.

"Lardy dardy" exclaimed Mrs. Pollard "poor young lady, I'll see to her at once sir."

She left the room and soon returned with an other servant and the two carried Helen to her bedroom where they bathed her face with cold water and put her to bed as carefully as possible.

97

" You'd best go for the doctor Mary " said Mrs. Pollard " say nothing to the young gentleman and be as quick as you can.

Meanwhile Cyril and Mr. Palsey sat down to their supper.

" Poor Helen " cried Cyril at last.

" Oh stop that tune do " cried Mr. Palsey " tell us what happened."

" It was all done as pre-arranged. I waited till the man was hanged and the yard emptied of people and while Mr. Winston was putting away the scaffold the blow was struck " said Cyril.

" By you ? "

" No."

" Who then ? "

" Oh that lout you saw at the door just now, he decided to do the job for £10, I had hard work to make him do it just at first " replied Cyril.

" Indeed " said Mr. Palsey " what was his name ? "

" Jack Jenkins " replied Cyril a terrific beggar and drunkard too I belive."

" Oh " laughed Mr. Palsey " and what plan did you adopt about the gun ? "

" I did'nt do that " responded Cyril " when Jenkins had done his part of the business, I got a knife, steeped it in red ink and laid it by Mr. Winston's side, as he was prostrated on the ground.

"And that will lead the police to belive it was suicide you think ? " asked Mr. Palsey.

" I think so " replied Cyril with a groan " at least that seemed to be the general opinion when the poor fellow was taken to the mortuary."

"Why do you say "poor fellow ? " asked Mr. Palsey.

" Because I do think he is a poor fellow and I'm sorry I ever did the thing " cried Cyril and he brought his fist down on the table with such force that the jug of beer toppled over and fell on the floor.

At that moment the door opened and Mrs. Pollard poked her head in "if you please sir " she said "we've thought fit to send for Dr. Poppet, and he's waiting in the hall."

"Very well " said Cyril with dignity "show him upstairs and when he has seen Miss Winston let him come and have a word with me."

" Miss Winston " cried Mrs. Pollard " why sir is she any relation to the poor hangman as was killed after the affair."

" Yes woman " cried Cyril hotly "she is his daughter, now go for pity's sake "

Mrs. Pollard hastily withdrew and commanded Dr. Poppet to follow her.

"Its a serious case sir " she said cheerily opening Helen's door "step this way please."

Dr. Poppet stepped that way and went over to Helens bed, where Mary the under servant was putting ointment on the wound.

"Hem" grunted the doctor seriously "not so bad as I feared, but very dangerous for all that, she must be kept very quiet Mrs. Pollard and must only take liquid food, she will probably awake by 5 or 6 o'clock and you may give her a little milk, "I'll call again tomorrow on my rounds, keep her head cool or fever of some kind may set in and affect the brain."

"Your instructions shall be carried out to the letter" said Mrs. Pollard and with that she led him down to talk with Cyril Sheene.

CHAPTER X

IN THE COURT OF JUSTICE

THE next morning Helen was sadly feverish, though quite sensible.

From the time she woke up 11-30 a.m. she never opened her lips.

She was very feverish and her brain very much upset.

Mr. Palsey decided not to tell Helen the fearful news till she was better and indeed it was a wise thing to do. Helen smiled and looked pleased when Cyril went to see her, but turned away in disgust when Mr. Palsey went near her.

"Helen dear" said Cyril "I am going out now, is there anything you would like me to buy for you?"

" No nothing " replied Helen " let me be alone, I want no one near me."

Cyril sighed, took up his hat and departed.

Entering the sitting room he found Mr. Palsey busy writing.

" James " said Cyril " I must go out now, will you come."

" No I cant " replied Mr. Palsey " I am very busy."

Cyril again gave a sigh of relief, and opening the front door went out.

The storm of the night before had quite subsided and the sun was shining brightly.

To tell the truth, Cyril was very glad to hear that Mr. Palsey could not go out, for he himself was going to the court of Justice to appear as witness concerning the death of Mr. Winston, which some of the detectives suspected to be murder and some suicide.

The court was densly crowded and in consequence very hot and stuffy.

Cyril forced his way through the crowd and seated himself in the witness box, where sat two other men, Mr. Porter the head warder of the prison and Dr. Slyn, both of whom had held conversation with Mr. Winston, an hour or so before his death.

" Not many witnesses for so serious a case " cried the judge in loud tones as he eyed the three desolate looking men.

Cyril was the first witness as he knew more

of the deceased than either the other two. He had to relate all he knew of Mr. Winston's past life and in conclusion the judge asked him if he thought Mr. Winston looked like commiting suicide when he went to hang Mr. Smith.

Cyril replied that Mr. Winston looked rather morbid on the day of the execution and otherwise no other change was visible.

The judge coughed, "summon the detectives" he cried.

The detectives (three in number) advanced.

"Now Mr. Slag" said the judge, addressing the leader of the three men, "what is your opinion of this terrible case, murder or suicide?"

Cyril waited open mouthed for the reply, his whole life depended on Mr. Slag's reply.

Mr. Slag evidently did not like giving his opinion in public and he hesitated before speaking.

"I say it was murder" cried one of the other detectives.

Cyril could have screamed with vexation.

"Are you aware Mr. Tix that your opinion was not asked" enquired the judge drily "Mr. Slag if you please" he added authoritivly.

"I say suicide most decidedly replied Mr. Slag "I am a trained detective my lord and am not likely to make a mistake, Mr. Rennet is also of my opinion."

"Very well" said the judge writing in his note book.

" I am convinced it is suicide and so the jury and you may go Mr. Slag, the case is with drawn where are Mr. Winston's relations who will bury the deceased ? "

A stir in the witness box and Cyril came forward " I will undertake to pay for the burial " he said.

" You ? " cried the astonished judge " who are you pray ? "

" My name is Cyril Sheene " replied Cyril getting very red " and I am the greatest friend poor Mr. Winston had, besides his daughter who I know is penniless.

" Very well " said the judge " you are a good benevolent man.

Little did the simple minded judge know, that the innocent looking person he addressed in such kind tones was the real murderer of Mr. Winston.

CHAPTER XI

HELEN'S RESOLVE

CYRIL SHEENE returned home to his lodgings quite satisfied with the conclusion the case had come to. Entering the sitting room, he found Mr. Palsey still busy writing, though the dinner was ready and fast getting cold.

" Still busy ? " cried Cyril, pulling off his gloves and sitting down to a tempting looking dinner of juicy well cooked mutton chops arranged against a mountain of frothy mashed potatoes.

"Yes I'm terrificly busy" responded Mr. Palsey tearing up a large sheet of foolscap as he spoke.

"Well lets have dinner now" responded Cyril sitting down as he spoke.

"Oh all right" replied Mr. Palsey, who was not the least hungry, "where have you been all the morning?"

"In court" responded Cyril absently gazing at the mutton chops.

"In court man!" cried Mr. Palsey "what do you mean?"

"I mean what I say" replied Cyril. "I was in court, acting witness in Mr. Winston's case."

"Really?" gasped Mr. Palsey "what is the result?"

"The case is withdrawn" replied Cyril feverishly, "they are convinced it is suicide."

"Thank goodness" ejaculated Mr. Palsey "then we are well out of the mess."

"Yes" answered Cyril and then vouchsafing no more the two men sat down to their dinner.

Half way through they were interupted by Mrs. Pollard, who came in in a great fluster.

"Please sir" she said in a hurry "Miss Winston seems so queer, she has got up and dressed herself and wishes to see you at once."

"My stars" screamed Cyril, forgetting in his

excitement what a gentleman he was and with that he rushed upstairs to Helen's bedroom.

He found Helen standing by the bed, her hands beating wildly against her heart and a hectic spot burning on her cheek.

She was completely dressed even to her grey travelling cloak which hung limply on her shoulders.

"Cyril," she cried wildly, "I am going home, I can bare this imprisonment no longer."

"Helen, my darling cried Cyril astounded by her words.

"Yes it is true" cried Helen again. "I shall go home now now—this instant why am I kept in ignorance of my father's death? I know who murdered him in spite of secrecy," she screamed," it was Mr. Palsey, that false villain below," "Helen cried Cyril," "how could it be Mr. Palsey, why I should know it if it was he, dont be absurd dear, get into bed again do you know you are very ill, and to go out would be madness."

"I dont care" screamed Helen, her eyes dilating and her cheeks burning.

"I shall go home, I tell you it was Mr. Palsey who murdered my father if you dont know it Cyril, I do so there,"

"Helen" said Cyril firmly "be calm and I will tell you about your poor father's death."

"Tell me" cried Helen and she sank exhausted into a chair.

"I fear" began Cyril "I greatly fear that your poor dear father commited —— had reasons for depriving himself of life."

"What!" cried Helen, starting to her feet, "you Cyril Sheene dare to insult me to my face, will you too turn, false, oh how dare you say my father commited suicide."

"I dare Helen because I know it" replied Cyril.

"You dont know it" screached Helen "oh Cyril," and the poor un nerved girl sank sobbing on the bed.

Hush Helen," cried Cyril stroking her ruffled hair," we wont talk about it any more, but indeed you can not go home today, it is impossible."

"I must I must" moaned Helen "oh Cyril let me go, I want to see Marshland."

"Helen, you cant go" replied Cyril "why do you want Marshland?

"Because she is my only true friend" cried Helen.

"Helen am I not a true friend" asked Cyril reproachfully.

"Yes Cyril you are" said Helen, "but do let me go."

Cyril remembering the doctors directions that Helen was to have everything she wanted, replied "very well Helen, you may go to-morrow, and now get back to bed and rest."

"No, no" said Helen "I must go tonight."

"But your father is to be burried today" replied Cyril.

"Never mind" cried Helen shaking her aching head, "It would break my heart to attend the funeral, I must go tonight.

"Very well" said Cyril "I will go with you, by the 8-40 train, but now do rest darling."

"Thank you, thank you Cyril" replied Helen gratefully and closing her eyes she fell into a heavy sleap."

CHAPTER XII

THE DISGUISE

CYRIL was greatly troubled about Helen's strange conduct; he knew it was not good for her to travel in her present condition, and then again it would do her just as much harm not to go as she desired it so much.

He went down to the sitting room and related all the story to Mr. Palsey and waited eagerly for a reply.

"Why man alive!" shrieked Mr. Palsey "this is greatest piece of luck we could possibly hope for."

"Luck?" cried Cyril "what do you mean?"

"Why don't you see?" said Mr. Palsey "it is impossible for Helen to travel alone, and therefore you and I must accompany her, and of course it will be the very chance of chances to rob the safe."

"But you cant go with her" replied Cyril "though of course I must."

"Why cant I go if you please?"

"For the simple reason that Helen suspects you to be guilty of murdering her father," replied Cyril, trying to appear unconcerned.

"What?" shrieked Mr. Palsey thumping his knees vigerously, "dont be an idiot, how can she suspect me?"

"Well she does" answered Cyril "but you may be quite easy, for she will not speak of it."

She'd better not" cried Mr. Palsey biting his moustache.

"But you see James, it is quite impossible for you to travel with us, so you had better wait and come by a later train, there is one at 9-12 I know" replied Cyril.

"No that wont do," said Mr. Palsey "it would upset my plans, besides making it too late to rob the safe with ease."

"What will you do then?" asked Cyril.
"I will disguise myself" returned Mr. Palsey "I have a heavy green ulster upstairs, which I know Miss Winston has not seen and grey slouch hat; and a false beard which I used when acting a play some time ago and if I put a little walnut juice upon my countenance I think I shall be sufficiently disguised at least to deceive Miss Winston."

"Capital" exclaimed Cyril, "put on the things now and see how you look."

Mr. Palsey rummaged in his portmanteau and produced the required articles. The beard was a trifle crumpled, but Cyril who was neat handed quickly combed it out and made it look as good as new.

Mr. Palsey then put on the ulster and big felt hat and attached the beard to his chin by a bit of elastic. Cyril then applied a few dabs of walnut juice to his face, and in a minute he was disguised into a fearce foreign looking man.

"Its a splended get up" said Cyril, eyeing the villain admiringly.

"I wont take it off" said Mr. Palsey opening his purse and taking out ten shillings "I will go straight to the station and wait there, give this money to Mrs. Pollard for me, it what I owe her for the lodgings you know.

"Very well" cried Cyril "but you'll have a long wait at the station."

"I know" said Mr. Palsey "but I can amuse myself with a few comic papers and a pipe."

"So with a hearty shake of the hands the two villains sealed the compact.

CHAPTER XIII

HOME AGAIN

CYRIL was very busy all that afternoon; he barely had time to attend Mr. Winston's funeral, which he did however for politeness sake.

It was not a grand funeral by any means and I think it would have broken Helen's heart to see the plain unvarnished coffin which her poor father's remains were deposited in.

When Cyril returned from the ceremony, he settled his accounts with Mrs. Pollard and then proceeded to pack his portmanteau, which piece of business did not take him very long.

He was about to depart from his room, when something lying upon the floor attracted his attention.

It was a water coloured painting of Mr. Winston.

How Cyril's heart smote him, as he gazed at those calm, stern features and mild blue eyes, with so much trust in their orbs.

He hastily shuffled the painting into his pocket, and with something between a groan and a sarcastic laugh, made a rapid retreat down the stair case.

Helen was waiting in the hall.

She looked a very different girl from the bright rosy faced Helen of a week ago.

Her cheeks were white and hollow save for one hectic spot and her great hazel eyes seemed too dark for her face. Her dark hair was limp and uncurled, and her lips were as ashy as her face. She looked a sad little picture, indeed, as she stood there in the hall, with her grey cloak loosly buttoned round her, and her new black crape hat contrasting queerly with her ghost-like countenance.

Cyril's heart of stone was quite touched as he saw her looking so vastly changed.

"Come Helen" he said carresingly as he patted her hair behind, "it feels like old times to be walking with you again."

"Perhaps it does to you" quoth Helen bitterly "but to me it is unbearable."

Cyril said nothing, but gently helped her down the steps. In an hours time they were at the station.

Helen sat on a seat to rest till the train came up, and Cyril went over to the bookstall, keeping close to a remarkably tall foreign looking gentleman who was laughing over Tit Bits.

"Come away," whispered Helen to Cyril "that man reminds me of the two faced villain Mr. Palsey."

"Helen" muttered Cyril between his teeth "be quiet do; please to remember that with all his villainy he is a perfect gentleman."

"Ah" said Helen "you too admit that he is a villain."

Cyril saw he had made a mistake and the hot blood rushed to his face.

"Dear me he said cooly "I am always blurting out things I dont mean."

Helen was beginning to see through him.

"Cyril" she said faintly "I hope you are not a villain too.

"Why of course I'm not" replied Cyril "come, here is the train."

Helen followed Cyril to a first class carriage, noticed that the foreign looking man, otherwise Mr. Palsey, jumped into a second class depart-ment and closed the door with a bang.

"This is a fast train" said Cyril as he got on to the seat.

"Indeed?" replied Helen, and with a deep drawn sigh she placed her bundle on the rack.

"Helen wont you eat your supper," asked Cyril "it is nearly nine o'clock, you must be hungry.

"Very well" replied Helen and she opened her bag.

"What have you got?" asked Cyril eargerly.

"Only a small pot of calf's foot jelly" answered Helen.

"Oh" said Cyril in a dissopointed tone, "why you ought to have had fruit and cold fowl."

"Dont speak to me of cold fowls" cried Helen in disgust and having finished her jelly she sank into repose.

The train was an express and reached Kenal-ham a little before 10-30.

Helen burst into tears as she stepped on to the platform "Oh how sad, how sad" she moaned.

The dog cart was waiting for them and Cyril jumped quickly in, helping Helen as he did so.

For ten minutes or more, the cart stopped, and Helen found herself once more on the threshold of her home.

CHAPTER XIV

THE ROBBERY

THE door was opened by Marshland who having heard the fearful news was attired in deep mourning.

"My darling Miss Helen!" cried the old servant.

"Oh Marshland" cried Hellen "I feel so terribly ill."

"Come to bed at once miss and you shall have some hot wine" said Marshland "step into the drawing room sir" she added seeing Cyril waiting in the passage.

"Goodnight Helen dear" cried Cyril, then turning to the servant he added "thank you I will rest for one moment, but I must go then, as I have a friend waiting for me in the town."

"Very well sir" said Marshland "you can let yourself out cant you?"

"Oh yes" cried Cyril and he betook himself to the drawing room.

As I have already mentioned, Helen was feeling weak and ill and her head ached as though it would split. Marshland put her to bed very carefully and gave her some hot wine to drink.

Once in between the beautiful cool sheets with the breeze blowing in at the open window stirring the dainty white muslin curtains, Helen dropped into a dull heavy sleep, but she was so restless that Marshland dared not leave her.

As the clock on the stairs struck 12.30, Helen seemed to grow quieter, so Marshland drew down the blind, snuffed the candle and went downstairs.

She bolted the hall door and peeped into the drawing room.

"I heard Mr. Sheene go some hours ago" she muttered "and all the windows are bolted, so off I go to bed to rest my weary limbs.

So the old woman went to her room, knocking at Glady's door as she went, to assure that she was going to bed, for Gladys who was highly nervous had insisted on this.

Helen slept heavily till about 2 o'clock in the morning, when she was awakened by some strange sounds below.

She sat up in bed and listened, the sounds

continued and feeling frightened she called Marshland.

But the old servant was asleep and for a little while the noises ceased. Helen thinking it was her fancy turned in her bed and fell into a doze. In less than 2 minutes she was awakened by the furious ringing of a bell.

For a moment her heart stood still and her very blood ran cold. Then in one desperate moment she recollected the sound of the bell.

Springing from her bed she flew to the door crying as she did so " the safe, the safe ! ! "

Wildly she flew down the passage her brain dazed her heart beating loudly.

Her eyes too dilated to see, and in flying along she struck her head against a tall old clock and would have fallen headlong downstairs, to certain death, but a pair of arms were hastily flung around her and in another moment two unconscios figures were lying motionless in the still dark passage with only the pale moonlight lighting up their rigid faces.

CHAPTER XV

" SETTLED."

MARSHLAND had not been awakened by the bell and so when she got up next morning at 6 o'clock, she was entirely innocent of the nights events. Putting on her apron she hastily went downstairs. Half way down the passage she caught sight of something white.

" Tut tut " she exclaimed " I wonder if those are my clean aprons or caps, they must have fallen from the beams." But here her wonderings were overun by the fact that the white things were no other than the prostrate bodies of Helen and Gladys.

Marshland uttered a stifled cry, but recovering her presence of mind she instantly raised Helen in her arms. Gladys had by this time quite recovered and was kneeling by her cousin on the floor.

" Raise yourself Miss Gladys " said Marshland "and help me take Miss Helen to her room."

Gladys rose directly and Helen was soon upon her bed once more.

She soon opened her eyes and fixed them on her cousin, "go away " she said calmly " I want to speak to Marshland."

Gladys left the room and Helen's calm manner changed to one of absolute fury.

Darting to her feet, she seized Marshland's shoulder, her white lips parted in feverish anxiety.

" The safe " she cried quick Marshland it has been robbed—I heard the bell—go and see quick, oh Marshland hurry—hurry."

Marshland had her doubts as to the robbery,

but to quiet Helen she went downstairs to ascertain.

Entering the drawing room to her great alarm she found the window wide open, and she knew she had shut and bolted it the night before.

Advancing in some consternation she saw the bolt had *not* been tampered with and her eyes wandered to the safe. Dragging back the curtain she perceived to her great horror that the gauze door was wide open and the black leather bag which contained all the money, gone.

"Oh Heavens" ejaculated the old woman "all the money gone, yes every brass farthing of it, my poor Miss Helen you'll have to go begging now and in sober earnest too."

It may here be mentioned that Mr. Winston had left a will leaving all his money to Helen, and the gold which that bag contained was all he had left, so that gone, Helen would have to set about to earn her own living. Mr. Winston had before his death written on a slip of paper "all this gold is bequeathed to my daughter Helen on the day when I shall be called upon to die." This he had sealed with his private seal and put at the bottom of the bag so that the thief (whoever he might be) had carried that signature with him.

Marshland lost no time in seeing what else had been robbed and found to her relief that the ivory box containing the valuable old jewils had not been touched.

Taking it in her trembling hand, she carried it to Helen's room. " Here miss " she said, see the jewils have not been touched but—but —her white lips refused to say any thing else, but Helen looked up the strain, " the money is gone, yes I knew it Marshland and I am left alone a beggar in this cruel, cruel world. All this she uttered in so calm a tone as to quite surprise Marshland.

" Dont say alone miss " cried the faithful servant, for I will be with you through thick and thin.

At that moment the door opened and Gladys announced that Mr. Sheene was waiting in the parlour, together with Mr. Palsey. Helen dressed herself quickly and leaning on Gladys's arm for support she entered the much disturbed drawing room.

Cyril was standing by the window, his hands in his trouser pockets looking desperatly ill.

Mr. Palsey looked as stern and hard as ever, and with his cigarette between his lips he appeared to be taking a general survey of the room.

" Good morning Miss Winston " he cried totally ignoring his future wife, " if you have any brains they ought to tell you what I am here about. Before Helen had time to reply Gladys stepped forward and laying her hand on

Mr. Palsey's arm looked in his face steadily and
said. " James, I dont know what you intend
saying but I am sure it is cruel and cutting and
I beg and pray of you to keep quiet whatever
it is. Helen is, as you know in great trouble
about her dear father, and added to that, a
robbery has been commited in the night, which
has deprived her of all the money which had
been left her and so she has now to earn her
own living——— "

" Hold " cried Cyril suddenly turning round,
" I have already heard of this terrible robbery
and though I have to grovell in the very ground,
Helen shall never have to earn her own living,
in the presence of everyone here I repeat my
words. I intend as soon as possible to take
Helen to London and marry her on the first
opportunity which presents itself ; I have " he
added, " though no one may know it, a private
bussiness in Holburn, which consists of a small
office in which I employ two clerks, my living
appartments are at the back of this office or
(home affair) as I generally call it, and mark
my words all of you here Helen would lead a
very happy life, and if my bussiness should
prosper I will go and live in Paris or Rome if
Helen should prefer it."

" Thank you Cyril " said Helen, " I will
spend one more week here to collect my belong-
ings and then only too gladly will I go with you
to your office. I have only one request to make."

" What is that ? " asked Cyril.

" A very simple one " replied Helen " only that Marshland should come with us and be our servant."

" Certainly," answered Cyril. " I shall be only too pleased, for the one servant I have is just leaving and I am sure Marshland will suit."

" Pardon me " said Mr. Palsey " I think Cyril, if you take my advice you will leave this wicked interfeering old woman behind I warn you she will be the plague of your life, for I myself have had experience of what she can do poking her nose into people's rooms, the meddling old cat."

" Mr. Palsey " said Helen calmly and with great dignity " perhaps you will allow Cyril to settle this matter, and if you will allow me to add, I would far rather be a meddling old cat, than a cruel hard hearted person who could murder a good innocent man for the sake of his money, and then could look the daughter of that man in the face with a cold unflinching gaze."

Gladys uttered a low scream and staggered towards the door ; she is loosing her head she sobbed, " going mad, and all through you James." For Gladys knew nothing of Helen's suspicions.

" No Gladys " replied Helen, " don't cry, for I am not loosing my head or going mad either, and you have my utmost pity for having a husband such as he."

" *Settled*."

But nothing could soothe poor Gladys and as Helen stooped to comfort her, Mr. Palsey took the opportunity of speaking to Cyril.

" You idiot " he hissed " look what you have led Helen up to, making her speak to me like that, now I doubt if Gladys will belive in me, and if she does not there will be an end to my rich marriage."

" I dont care " said Cyril, for he truly felt he had the upper hand, " I consider it would be a very good thing if Miss Lincarrol does not marry you for she is too good a girl to be joined with a low villain like you."

" Very well " cried Mr. Palsey savagely " as you evidently consider yourself a saint, (though you did help me in the murder and other matters too) perhaps it will be better for both of us if we seperate at once.

I have my half of the money and you have yours, so that is all settled, you can take Helen to London and marry her and I will take Gladys to Norfolk where all her relations live and marry her when I get settled and the less we hear of each other the better, that is my opinion and I hope it suits you.

" It does " replied Cyril calmly " let us tell the girls and the sooner you and Gladys get packed off the better for I must stay here another week with Helen."

" Gladys " cried Mr. Palsey firmly " get up at once and stop crying."

" Gladys dried her eyes and sat up.

" Look here " continued Mr. Palsey, "you and I are going back to Norfolk this evening as soon as we can mannage it, and Mr. Sheene intends stopping another week with Miss Winston till he goes to London and remember the less you and she hear of one another the better ; you will be much better for the loss of her company and your relations too would much rather you left here, it is taking effect on your health my dear, so be ready to start by 6 o'clock this evening and I will call for you ; you and Helen will have plenty of time to say your last adieu before that ; is that settled ? " he added turning to Cyril.

" Quite " replied Cyril.

Gladys broke into heart broken sobbing but being used to obey she ran quickly upstairs to collect her things.

With a cry Helen ran to Cyril and put her arms round his neck.

Mr. Palsey bit his lips and turning to the window he turned over the past events in his mind and he thought how very well he had managed that last little bit of business.

CHAPTER XVI

BOUND FOR NORFOLK

LET us now return to Gladys.

Arrived at her bedroom she began to collect her various articles of clothing in a hazy and disturbed manner, every now and then sitting down to burst into a terrible fit of weeping.

It took her over half an hour to pack up, and then having bathed her burning face, she began to feel very hungry.

Finding a few biscuits in a tin, she lost no time in eating them and then she rang her bell.

To her supprise Helen came to the door instead of Marshland.

"Oh dear Gladys" cried Helen kindly "I am so very sorry that you are going."

"Oh Helen," sobbed Gladys "it nearly breaks my heart to think of it, and we may not even write to each other."

"Dont say that" cried Helen, "if ever I can manage it I'll always send you a note privately, for I shall never forget Gladys that you saved my life."

Gladys could not speak for crying.

"Now Gladys" said Helen "do stop crying or you will be ill, did you want anything when you rang just now."

"Oh yes please" replied Gladys "if I might have something to eat, I am so very hungry."

"Certainly, dear" said Helen and she darted downstairs, soon to return with a plate of well cut ham and a couple of poached eggs and a comforting cup of coffee.

Having spread this out, she sat down to watch Gladys eat it.

The poor girl looked very worn out and tired and great red and black lines encircled her blue eyes. "oh Helen" she said at last "do tell me what you meant by speaking so strongly to James just now.

The tears came into Helen's eyes, "dont ask me Gladys dear" she said, some day I will contrive to let you know by letter but I cant tell you now."

A silence followed and then Helen spoke again, "do you know" she said. "I am very glad things have turned out like this I shall be happy too and perhaps you will forget all about me and all this misery."

"Oh Helen" cried Gladys "I will never forget you it will be impossible."

"I dont know" said Helen "you see its like this, although we shall write to each other (for my mind is made up on that score) when once you are happy, though you will not exactly forget *me*, you will forget this misery at parting and so you will be able to think of me without pain or regret, and it will be like a wound which though healed over is still to be seen, do you under stand?"

"Yes dear Helen" said Gladys "there is certainly truth in what you say, but do you think we shall either of us be happy again?"

"Yes" said Helen with a smile, "I do, light is certainly breaking through the darkness after all Gladys"

Ah Helen!, happily for you that you can see the bright light appearing, but there are dark clouds gathering in the distance which you do not see but which nevertheless are coming nearer and nearer and will soon burst over your head and extinguish the sunshine and the light.

The dreary morning passed away at last and the afternoon followed suit. A quarter to six found Gladys and Helen taking a last farewell in the drawing room before Mr. Palsey arrived.

"Oh Helen shall we ever meet again, sobbed Gladys.

"Hush hush" said Helen "dont cry Gladys and let me give you some advice before you go. Dont sob or show any emotion when you bid me goodbye and if afterwards Mr. Palsey should mention me to you be quite calm and show him you do not care, when next we meet I'll tell you my reasons and be sure they're good ones."

Voices were heard at the front door and going into the hall, they found Mr. Palsey and Cyril talking and a carriage waiting at the gate.

"Goodbye Miss Lincarrol" said Cyril as he took her hand "I am sorry you have to go."

"Not at all" said Gladys brightly "goodbye Mr. Sheene, thanks for all your kindness."

Here Mr. Palsey interposed "goodbye Miss Winston" he said raising his hat.

Helen drew herself up and gave him a look (such a one as once seen never forgotten) and then turning to her friend said, "well goodbye Gladys, a pleasant journey to you dear."

Goodbye Helen" said Gladys bravely and calmly and without a break in her voice.

"I hope you will enjoy yourself in London."

Mr. Palsey looked astounded, he had expected a loud fit of crying at least.

"Wont you say goodbye to me Miss Winston he asked sheepishly

"No cried Helen in a loud voice, "it was an evil day for you Mr. Palsey when my good father asked you to his house."

Mr. Palsey jumped into the open fly and put his bag beside him.

Helen stood on the steps waving her hand with tears in her eyes, while Gladys, for the sake of the friend she loved, sat erect and tearless in the carriage which soon wheeled her away from "Beach Dale" and its occupants.

CHAPTER XVII

THE OFFICE

LEFT alone in the dreary little cottage, a sense of utter lonliness came over Helen. She truly felt as though the one spark of happiness in her life had faded. Sitting down in an arm chair, she took up some crochet and tried to do a little work before sunset.

In a few minutes Cyril entered, fresh from a country walk.

" Ah Helen " he cried " you're busy I see."

" No I'm not " replied Helen sadly " did you want me for anything ? "

" Well I was thinking it might be as well to go and see the autioneer, Mr. Graham," replied Cyril " you see all this furniture must be sold and a week is but a short time to settle everything."

" Yes I presume that would be best " said Helen with a sigh " where does this Mr. Graham live ? " " Not a very long way off " replied Cyril " 49 Eastern Grove is his address "

" Oh yes I know " said Helen " when shall we start " ?

" Now, if you like " said Cyril "

" Very well," and Helen tossed away her crochet and put on her hat.

It did not take very long to reach Eastern Grove, a pretty little street at the end of Kenelham. Helen stood by while Cyril arranged matters to his own taste. At last all was settled and Mr. Graham politely promised to be round Beach Dale by 9 o'clock the next morning.

The next three days were busy ones indeed for Helen. All day she was flying up and downstairs, from attic to kitchen placing the furniture to be sold in lots and keeping what she wanted to take, in her own bedroom. Marshland helped all she could but being old and stiff she could do little but sit in the kitchen and moan at the loss of her beloved master's goods.

Friday came at last (the day Cyril had arranged for starting) and Helen was up early taking a last look at the rooms, garden walks etc., that she loved.

It was a boiling hot day and they had to start in the middle of the heat.

A large waggon came to the door wherein all the odd pieces of furniture were packed and the trunks and boxes being put on the top of that, Helen and Marshland got a small wooden bench which they put at the door of the waggon for, as Marshland truly remarked "Air was better than comfort," and there they seated themselves to drive to the station—Cyril had gone on to take the tickets and see about a comfortable carriage.

It was two o'clock by the time they reached Holburn.

Cyril jumped out, ordered a hansom while Helen attended to the luggage.

"Now Marshland" cried Cyril "you and Miss Helen will kindly get into this hansom and I'll tell the man where to drive to, I have a bussiness matter to settle, but you can tell the servant girl I'll be in to tea"

Helen and Marshland got hastily into the hansom, to the old servant's inexpressible delight who had never ridden in anything but the customary Kenelham dog cart, and the waggon she had recently quitted. Helen however was too tired to notice anything and the new sights and sounds had no charm for her country eyes.

Presently the cab stopped at a small dreary looking office with the name Sheene & Co : in guilt letters on the window. Two men evidently the clerks, were watching with intense excitement the descent of the two ladies from the cab, their faces being pressed upon the iron blind of the office window.

Helen went up the steps and timidly rang the "visitors bell".

It was soon answered by a rough untidy looking servant girl, with no cap and a dirty cotton dress, whom Marshland eyed with intense disgust.

"Are you Mr. Sheene's ladies?" asked the girl.

"Yes" replied Helen "and Mr. Sheene wished me to say you were to show us to our rooms at once, he himself will not be in till tea time."

"All right" responded the servant "step in and follow me."

She then led the way down a narrow passage past the home affair, till she came to a door which she flung open, announcing it was the sitting room.

"You wont want your bedrooms yet awhile" she said "because they're not ready."

"Oh pray dont trouble" said Helen.

"Very well" replied the girl and she went off closing the door behind her.

"The slovenly creature" cried Marshland "Mr. Sheene has evidently had no practice in choosing his domestics.

The room in which they found themselves was rather small and very stuffey, the window being tight shut and the blind down. A red carpet adorned the floor a common deal table with a check cloth stood in the middle of the room, and three chairs were carefully arranged round it. A leather armchair was by the fire-place adorned by a crochet antimicassa, and a sofa of the same discription was by the window. The mantle piece was furnished with two glass vases, and a clock, and a large photograph of Cyril and his two clerks. A sideboard was by the door covered with a clean cloth, a parrafin lamp, two trays and a bowl of lavender.

"What do you think of it?" asked Helen

after she had opened the window and taken off
her hat and gloves.

"Humph" said Marshland looking round
"pretty fair, but law Miss Helen, comparing
it with your father's dainty little parlour its a
mere scullery."

"Yes" said Helen "but dont let us hurt
poor Cyril's feelings, no doubt he likes it."

"No doubt" replied Marshland.

By 5 o'clock Cyril came in, very hot but
happy for all that. "Well Helen" he said
what do you think of your future abode"?

"Oh its very nice" answered Helen.

"Well let us ring for tea" cried Cyril "you
will take your meal with us tonight Marshland,
but tomorrow you will find your place in the
kitchen with Alice the maid, who will do all
the hard work while you preside."

Marshland looked pleased but said nothing.

Alice brought in the tea, and the three made
it off shrimps and bread and butter and by
that time Helen was pleased to go to bed,
quite pleased with her first day in London.

Helen's bedroom was at the top of a very
steep staircase and it was even more stuffy than
the sitting room. A rather dirty white blind
hung in the window, which Marshland instantly
tore down, "the filthy rag" she exclaimed
"never mind Miss Helen, in a few weeks, I'll
have this fit for a lady and the sitting room too
for that matter.

The iron bed stead was of the collapsible kind and Helen had to prop it up with empty trunks in order to get a night's rest, but what with the squalling of the office cats and the noise of the clerks and servants below, it was in the small hours of the morning before either she or Marshland got a wink of sleep.

CHAPTER XVIII

IMPROVEMENTS

It was 8 o'clock, the following morning when Helen was awakened by hearing a loud dispute outside her door between Marshland and Alice Grimstone (the maid).

Glancing at her watch, Helen jumped out of bed and began her toilet and half way through she was interrupted by Alice bouncing in announcing it was gone 8 o'clock and would she (Helen) care about any water for washing. Helen declared she would, upon which she was presented with a can of hot water and a clean towel, soap already having been provided.

Having placed the last hair pin in her knob and fastenned her white blouse, Helen went down to the sitting room, where a smell of hot coffee and fried bacon greated her nose.

" Ah this is Marshland's cooking " thought

Helen as she raised the cover of the dish. A great improvement was also visible in the room itself. It had been well dusted and swept and a few london flowers adorned the mantle shelf, a clean white curtain hung in the window, and Helen's work box and other little articles lay about the room, making it look far more home like than on the preceding evening.

Cyril (Helen had heard) rose very late, so she was forced to partake of her breakfast alone.

As soon as she had finnished, she rang the bell and ordered a fresh meal to be got ready for Cyril, for she really wished to please him and hoped in a few days time to have the house really nice.

Then Helen thought she would go out and buy a few things, so calling Marshland she said

" I am going out now Marshland, and lunch will be at 1.30 if you please. Mr. Sheene likes high tea at 7 and in the future we will follow this rule, breakfast at 9. lunch at 1.30, high tea at 7, Wine and biscuits 9.30."

"Very well miss " replied Marshland I'll see to it "

"Yes " said Helen and do make that girl work for pity's sake, she is so lazy "

"That she is miss " replied Marshland " She'll find her work set now I've come ".

Helen laughed "very well " she replied

" I'll be in soon. I only want to buy a chicken and a yard or so of muslin for curtains."

So going out, Helen hailed a hansom and got proudly in, much to the envy of Netherby and Wilson (the two clerks) to whom she had not yet been introduced.

And so day followed day and Helen always found plenty to do. She was a first rate house keeper and Cyril treasured her accordingly. Marshland too made vast improvements in the lower regons. Alice was made to work hard and keep herself tidy.

A bright yellow canary was purchased, and hung in the sitting room window to Helen's great delight, and she had no time to be unhappy. Cyril seemed to prefer being engaged so the marriage was put off, and Helen was once more light hearted and merry and her gay laugh might often be heard as she chatted cheerily to the clerks or played comic songs on the little harmonium.

And yet no one is there to warn Helen of the approaching danger and misery.

CHAPTER XIX

THE SILVER TEAPOT

TIME sped on and nothing happened to alarm or upset Helen untill a certain October morning.

She had just commenced her breakfast, when

in came Cyril attired in his best black suit and stiff collar.

" Why Cyril " cried Helen " how very early you are."

" Yes I am " responded Cyril triumphantly " I'm going to see a friend who lives in Piccadilly and I doubt if I shall be back before 10 or 11 tonight'"

" Really " ? said Helen, " well make a good breakfast or you'll be quite done up."

Cyril made a hearty meal and then went to the front door to see if the weather promised to be fair ; it looked rather gloomy, but no rain fell. As though a sudden thought had struck him, Cyril turned round and entered the office.

" Netherby " he cried sharply " who's afternoon out is it, your's or Wilson's ?

" It is Mr. Wilson's sir " replied Netherby.

" Then see he does'nt have it " said Cyril shortly " I have my own reasons for wishing you both to remain at home today, and dont forget the office is in your charge today Netherby ; admit no gossiping women or tradesmen."

" No sir " replied the clerk. Cyril turned to leave the office, nearly knocking Helen over as he did so. " Are you off " ? she enquired " put on your overcoat dear, it is very chilly."

" All right " said Cyril and he reached his blue melton from the peg.

As Helen was helping him on with his coat she noticed something silver sticking out of the breast pocket.

" Why whatever is this ? " she asked in supprise. " it looks like the best silver tea pot."

" Best silver tea pot ! " cried Cyril scornfully, as though a man cant carry his cigarette case about with him."

But he looked uncommonly angry for all that and Helen had seen and felt quite enough to convince her that it was the best tea pot and she felt her heart turn sick as she closed the front door after Cyril's retreating figure.

CHAPTER XX

THE PAWN TICKET

HELEN's heart was beating fast, as she went back to the sitting room, " oh dear " she cried sitting down on the sofa " whatever is Cyril up to I wonder it *was* a tea pot I know and it was wrapped in cotton wool too for it felt soft, I do hope he is up to no tricks."

Finding nothing to do Helen sat down to strum on the harmonium, but this did not soothe her spirits and she wandered about the room till her eye fell on a little white ticket lying on the hearthrug. She could not bear to see paper lying on the floor, so she hastily picked it up, and before tossing it into the fire she looked at it well to make sure it was nothing important.

Helen knew enough to see at first glance it was a pawn ticket for a valuable silver sugar basin worth £1 10. 0.

Her cheeks grew white as she read it and she felt her fingers growing stiff. "Of course" she cried "its as plain as day light, Cyril has pawned the best sugar baisen for a few trumpery shillings, oh I'm sure he is getting into bad company" and she commenced to weep. "And I know he means to pawn the tea pot too." But this was only the beginning of another long series of troubles for poor Helen, but happily for her she did not know that or it might have driven her mad.

CHAPTER XXI

AN UNEXPECTED VISIT

HELEN's weeping had given her a headache and she was taking a doze on the sofa, when angry voices were heard at the front door. The voices were those of Mr. Netherby and a young lady evidently in great distress.

Helen came to the passage to hear what was the matter "I tell you I've had orders from

Mr. Sheene to let no gossiping women inside this office" cried Mr. Netherby. "But I'm not a gossiping woman" said the lady in agitation.

And how do I know that"? enquired Mr. Netherby. "I tell you I am a hater of gossip" screamed the lady "and here it is pouring rain and you have the audacity to keep me waiting at the front door, when I ask to see the lady of the house."

"There is no lady of this house" said Mr. Netherby "except Mrs. Marshland and she rules it with a firm hand"

"I want to see Miss Winston" cried the lady now almost in tears.

Here Helen interrupted, "Mr. Netherby" she said "If this lady wishes to see me, kindly let her in at once."

"I've got the master's orders not to" replied Netherby firmly.

"Insolent person"! cried Helen "obey me at once, open the door".

Netherby was alarmed and opening the door he fled into the office leaving his mistress to admit her guest if she would.

"Can I do anything for you my good lady"? asked Helen opening the door wide.

With a cry the lady flung herself into Helen's arms, saying "oh Helen Helen, how very glad I am to see you."

"Why Gladys" cried Helen "how came you here"? "Oh its a long story" said

Gladys (for it was she) "if I may come in, I'll tell it to you."

"Yes do" said Helen "stay the whole day if you will, for Cyril is out and I am entirely alone" So saying Helen led the way to the sitting room, where Gladys soon divested herself of her dripping cloak and hat, and sat down by the fire to warm herself. "How dreadfully wet you are" said Helen as she shook out Glady's cloak.

"I had to walk all the way from Holburn station" replied Gladys "there were no cabs to be seen" "Dear dear" said Helen "I hope you wont take cold."

"Not I" laughed Gladys "and now Helen dear if you are ready I'll tell you why I came here."

"Yes do" pleaded Helen drawing her chair to the fire. "It is a long story" mused Gladys gazing into the fire, as though she could see the events of the past three months of her life written there in letters of red and gold. "as you know Helen, when I left Kenelham I went with James straight to Norfolk, where my parents and relations live. James and I stayed there for, say three weeks, and during that time I was perfectly happy. I did not write to you as I didn't know your address, I presume you did'nt know mine. Well at the end of these three weeks James got an invatation to go and stay with some people in Brighton and he asked me to go too I was glad to do so as I had never been to that part at all. So it was arranged for me to go and we started. We had not been there a week when a marked change came over James. He grew white and thin and seemed so terribly nervous about the smallest thing. Men were constantly calling to see him and after their visits he looked even worse. It was not a large house where we stayed, and my room was next to his. He went to bed very late and I fancy he slept badly. I constantly heard him moan and walk about his room, and what terrified me so much was he used to talk about murders and robberies. So I took to listening to him, by putting my bed close to the wall. And I believe he found it out, for he took to ill treating me, that is to say he was not kind, and he called me horrible names. I felt it very much indeed and it must have made me look ill, for Mrs Martin (the hostess) said she thought the sea air did not agree with me and advised James to take me to some place where I had not been before. Accordingly we arranged to take a small house in Richmond for a few months till I got better. There it is we are living now. We have most comfortable rooms in a nice house overlooking the terrace gardens. Our landlady is a very good soul, and though I am much better for the change, James is not, he remains the same. All at once I remembered what you said to him that day about a murder. So I resolved to come and find out where you lived. I told James I wanted a whole day to do as I liked and I took a train for Holburn and I was directed where to go to, and here I am arrived in the very knick of time, just as Mr. Sheene is off for the day and you are quite alone to answer any questions I put to you."

During the latter part of Glady's story Helen had grown very white and she now paced the room in breathless agitation.

" What is it Helen "? enquired Gladys.

" Yes I knew I was right " muttered Helen half aloud " it is true too true alas ! but my revenge is at hand."

" Helen do sit down " cried Gladys " you look quite scared, I hope my story has not frightened you."

" Frightenned me, No " cried Helen loudly " you have only confirmed doubts which have been lingering in my brain for month's past ".

" Doubts, what doubts ". asked Gladys.

Oh Gladys " cried Helen bursting into tears " thank goodness you came to me today, for you may yet be saved from a terrible misfortune."

" For pity's sake Helen speak out " cried Gladys " you talk like a tragedian Gladys " said Helen " did you say that Mr. Palsey talked about murders and robberies ? "

" Yes " replied Gladys sadly " he certainly made use of those two words ".

"Shall I tell you why?" asked Helen "I shall be much obliged if you will" answered Gladys.

"Mr. Palsey's conscience has begun to trouble him" replied Helen.

"Oh Helen what do you mean?" cried Gladys wildly.

"Simply this" said Helen "you know when my poor father died, people said it was suicide."

"Yes, but I never belived that" said Gladys with marked descision.

"Evidently the detectives have found out their mistake" replied Helen "you say, men are constantly calling on Mr. Palsey."

"Yes" replied Gladys "they are, but Helen whatever do you mean."

"Gladys" said Helen, "don't hate me for what I am going to tell you; I only do it because I love you and wish to save you, it is a blessing you came here today, I suppose in another week you would have married Mr. Palsey but you wont now, for the man you call your lover is the murderer of my father."

Gladys gave a loud groan and sank helpless to the floor.

Helen ran to lift her up and after dashing some water on her face was happy to see her open her eyes.

"Gladys, dear Gladys" she cried "I should not have told you."

"Yes, yes" said Gladys faintly, "you did

quite right, only it was such a shock to me, after beliving in him all these months."

" Of course it is " replied Helen soothingly " thank goodness I shall never have cause to doubt Cyril's honour."

" Oh Helen what shall I do ? " moaned poor Gladys " to think of going back to sleep in the house with a villian like him " he might try to murder me in the night."

" Why not stay here a few nights till you think of some plans " suggested Helen " we have heaps of room."

" Oh no no " cried Gladys desperately " I dare not vex James like that and besides Mr. Sheene would not have me in his house."

" Oh Gladys " cried Helen " he would be only too pleased to be of help to you."

" No he would not " said Gladys " he hates me."

" Gladys ! " screamed Helen " how can you ? "

" It is true " said Gladys " and I will tell you why."

Helen gave a snort of disgust but she listened attentively for all that.

" You see " said Gladys " I had to walk from Holburn Station as you know and it took me some time as I did not know the way ; I had just caught sight of this office from the opposite side of the road and was going to cross, when the door opened and Mr. Sheene himself came out, he did not see me at first, he appeared to be looking at the sky, but the moment he caught sight of me his face darkened directly, he looked at me for a minute with posative hatred in his eyes, and then turning round he went into the office, to give an order, I presume that order was that no women were to be let in, because the instant I asked to see you, I was furiously assaulted by a presuming clerk, who called me a gossiping woman, and no end of horrid names."

"Oh" said Helen rather crossly "I think you must be mistaken, but all the same if you wont stay the night, you wont,"

"I really can not," replied Gladys.

"Did Cyril speak to you when he came out again?" enquired Helen.

"Dear me no" replied Gladys "I took jolly good care he shouldn't, so I bolted into a confectioners to escape him, where I had to go to the trouble of buying a bath bun ; but anything was better than not seeing you."

"Dont be sarcastic" returned Helen hotly "you dont treasure me as much as that."

"Dont I ?" cried Gladys "when I wanted to see you, I was not going to be snubbed by an insolent clerk, I would have braved him even if you had not come though I thank my stars you did come all the same, it is very degrading to be seen arguing with a common city clerk."

"So I should imagine" replied Helen "I can't say I have ever been in the same strait

myself; I am on very good terms with both
Netherby and Wilson."

"Are you?" said Gladys "which do you
like best."

"Well you see Netherby is rather alarmed
at me" replied Helen " since I blew him up
for attempting to touch the organ without
leave ; but then he is more to be trusted than
Wilson, who thinks nothing of breaking his
word, telling stories etc : Cyril has often
thought of dismissing him only he is very sharp
and a good writer I belive."

"Well Helen can you suggest any plan for
me" asked Gladys "I cant marry James that
is certain, but I cant go home and tell him that
to his face can I?"

"Hardly" said Helen "if I were you I
should go home, and dont say a word to Mr.
Palsey, and write at once to your parents,
telling them all you know as soon as you get a
reply write and let me know and I will endevour
to come up and see you and we can arrange
some plans ; of course get Mr. Palsey out of
the way before you ask me."

"Oh yes" said Gladys "that is easily done,
but mind you dont tell Mr. Sheene you have
seen me today nor dont tell him you are coming to see me either."

"Oh no" replied Helen " I'll merely say I
am going to Richmond for a trip, he does not
know you live there."

" Then that is settled " replied Gladys with a sigh of relief " what time to you expect Mr. Sheene home ? "

" Not till quite late " said Helen " you must stay to lunch."

" Thank you " said Gladys " I shall be delighted."

So Helen rang the bell and when Alice answered it she ordered dinner for two in a most bussiness like way.

Having made a good lunch, Gladys put on her things and got ready to start.

" You must not walk again " said Helen " I'll call a hansom," so saying she opened the front door and gave a soft whistle. In a minute a hansom drove up to the door and Helen helped her friend in.

" Goodbye Gladys " she said " dont forget to write and let me know directly you here from Norfolk and I'll come up if I can."

" No, I'll be sure to write " responded Gladys " thank you so much Helen for all your kindness," and with a wave of her hand Gladys was driven rapidly away in the direction of Holburn Station, while Helen returned to the sitting room, a great weight lifted from her heart.

CHAPTER XXII

CYRIL'S RETURN AND THE PROMISED VISIT

It was past ten before Cyril returned home very wet and cross into the bargin.

Helen saw at a glance what she might expect, so she carefully made up the fire and set a nice hot supper on the table.

" How tired you look dear " she said as she helped him off with his over coat.

" Well I suppose I do " replied Cyril crossly.

" Did you find your friend at home? " enquired Helen.

" Yes I did " said Cyril hastily pouring out his beer.

" Well that's all right " said Helen cherrily putting a lump of coal on the fire.

" No it's not all right " replied Cyril " for pity's sake leave that fire alone, I'm not going to sit up all night.

Helen smiled " have you a tooth ache dear " she asked.

" No I've not " said Cyril " look here Helen, have you seen a little card about the floor to-day? "

" Yes dear " replied Helen " a little Xmas card, that Mrs. Gingham sent you last year."

" Oh yes " said Cyril, trying to look as though that was what he meant " where did you put it? "

" In the desk dear " replied Helen producing a faded little card, which in an ordinary moment Cyril would have tossed into the fire, but now he carefully placed it in his note book.

" By the way Helen," said Cyril " I find I must go to Piccadilly again tomorrow as I did not get through my bussiness today, have breakfast at 8.30 will you ? "

" Yes dear " replied Helen, and after saying goodnight to him, she put out the lamp, taking care to drop the pawn ticket, (which had been in her pocket all this time) on the hearth rug, where she had found it.

Helen slept very soundly indeed and she therefore was awake early. She got dressed quickly, and went down to the sitting room.

Pulling up the blind she glanced quickly round the room. The ticket still lay where she had dropped it ; Cyril had evidently not been down.

By a quarter to 9 he made his appearance.

" Now Helen hurry up with the tea ! " he cried " it is getting late."

"That's no fault of mine " replied Helen quietly " time will fly you know."

" Who said it would'nt ? " asked Cyril snappishly, sitting down in the grumps.

" Why on earth does'nt Marshland send up the silver tea pot ? " asked Helen artfully " I hate this old brown china concern ; I'll ring for the other ; and the sugar bowl too."

" No, no please dont," cried Cyril nervously " I really cant wait."

" Well if it is'nt sent up tonight I shall make a row about it " replied Helen crossly " I cant bear keeping the silver for special occasions."

Cyril did not notice the ticket so Helen went and picked it up, " what's this ? " she asked curiously.

" What's what " asked Cyril turning sharply round.

" This little card " said Helen.

" Oh that's mine " replied Cyril " I'll put it in my pocket if you give it here."

Helen handed it over, " it looks exactly like a pawn ticket does'nt it ? " she asked.

" Yes, its not unlike one " replied Cyril.

" No not at all " said Helen, " in fact when I read it yesterday, I thought it was uncommonly like one."

Cyril turned a ghastly white and flew into the hall to get his hat.

" Ha ha my dear " thought Helen " I've found out your little game," but never the less she followed him innocently into the hall," dear Cyril she exclaimed " I hope my thinking that ticket like a pawn one has not upset you ; of course it is awfully foolish of me I know."

" Yes I know it is " replied Cyril cooly, " I may say more than foolish."

Helen laughed " you wont be so late today I presume," she said.

"No I dont think so" said Cyril, "I may be home by three o'clock today."

"Very well" replied Helen "dont hurry on my account, and with a giggle she opened the door and watched Cyril safely down the street, "yes my boy" she thought I dare say I'm cleverer than you take me for, any how I know where you're off to now and I wish you luck" and with a sigh Helen entered the office.

"Netherby" she cried "a word with you if you please."

The clerk shuffled quickly to his feet and followed Helen into the passage.

"Now look here" said Helen firmly "did Mr. Sheene ask if any ladies entered the office yesterday."

"Netherby looked uneasily at the floor and kicked up the oil cloth.

"Speak up" cried Helen loudly, "and dont tear my carpets please."

"Well miss" said Netherby nervously "he did mention something of the kind last night."

"Oh he did, did he" screamed Helen "and what did you say?"

"Well miss I did'nt tell a story" said Netherby "I said not that I knew of because you see miss, I did'nt look to see if you let the lady in or not after I went into the office."

"Thank you Netherby" said Helen "you have done me a great service," and she pressed a sovereign into the trembling hand of the clerk.

Entering the sitting room she found Alice waiting with a telegram in hand "its for you miss" she said "and the reply is prepaid."

Helen tore it open ; it ran thus :

"Have heard from Norfolk, come directly.
                                    Gladys.

Seizing a pencil Helen wrote the following answer :

            "Will try to come tomorrow.

Helen giving it to Alice she told her to take it at once.

"Poor Gladys" she thought, "I must manage to get to Richmond tomorrow what ever happens."

The morning passed and Cyril was home to lunch in very good spirits.

"Do you know Cyril" said Helen "I've often longed to go to Richmond for a trip, it must be such a nice place."

"Have you dear?" said Cyril, "well I must endevour to take you one day."

"Could you take me tomorrow?" asked Helen knowing he had an engagement on that day.

"No, not tomorrow" said Cyril "why?"

"Well there is a special matinee I wanted to see" said Helen "I promise you I'd be back by 8 in the evening."

"All right" said Cyril "you may go if you

wish it ; be back early you know " here's the
money for your seat."

" Oh thank you " cried Helen " this is jolly
I shall have a rare time I expect. I shall go
there by the 9-12. You know and have a
whole day of it."

" Very well " replied Cyril with a laugh, and
kissing him soundly Helen ran upstairs to
dream happily over the coming event.

CHAPTER XXIII

HELENS HAPPY DAY

THE sun was streaming in at Helen's little
window, when she opened her eyes at 7.45
the following morning. Jumping out of bed
with a happy feeling about her Helen lifted
the lower sash of her window and lent out as
far as possible. The October morning air
blew chill against her lightly clad figure but
the sun was high in the Heavens and with a
sigh of relief she closed her casement and
began to get dressed.

" Let's see " she said opening her ward-robe
and taking a view of the garments therein
" I'll put on my best dress if Marshland has
mended the skirt " and so saying Helen shook
out a pretty tweed dress trimmed with a deep
pointed collar of scarlet velvit and cuffs to match
and proceeded to button it on herself.

Here she was interupted by a loud knocking at the door and Alice thrust her head in saying " If you please miss, Mr. Sheene says he dont know what train you're a-going to Richmond by because its going on for 9 and the breakfast is almost cold ".

" Oh dear " cried Helen hastily pinning on her hat, " I'll be down directly ; what a time I've been dressing " she added. Seizing her gloves, umbrella, and little gold bracelet, she dashed downstairs and into the sitting room where a cold unpleasant breakfast greeted her, but Cyril was in a very good temper and that was just what was wanted, thought Helen as she gulped down her cold tea.

" Here " cried Cyril tossing her a sovereign on the table, " that's a little contribution towards your pleasure trip ".

" Oh thanks Cyril " cried Helen joyfully " but do you mind dear if I dont go to the theatre ; I have thought it over and I think I'll walk about the town, go to the terrace gardens, see the churches, and perhaps go on the river if it is fine, or if not go for a drive ".

" Allright " replied Cyril carelessly " I think you're much wiser myself, I always thought it was silly to go to the theatre ; if you go to the town for a day you naturally wish to see it thoroughly, as of course it is'nt a place you're ever likely to go to again.

" Exactly " replied Helen with a smile,

153

"now Cyril I'm off; when do you start for Picadilly"?

"Not till 10.30" replied Cyril, "now hurry up or you'll be late; be back by eight wont you" and he strode to the front door with her, where a hansom stood waiting.

"Goodbye" cried Helen waving her hand to him: "Goodbye" replied Cyril "I'm so glad you're going to have a happy day" And as she drove off, Cyril thought what a bright pretty little blossom she looked with her bright eyes and rosy cheeks, compared to many of the ugly looking men who adorned the boxes of the London cabs.

PART II

CHAPTER XXIV

A CRISIS

To do Cyril justice, it will be only fair to say that he experienced no slight pang at parting with his pretty little future wife for one day only, for, cruel and hardened as he had become, he had a deep and undying love for Helen in the bottom of his heart.

"What a dear she is," he muttered to himself, as the hanson disappeared round the corner, "and what a beast I am; I've deceived her all these months and I am still doing so. If it hadn't been for that villain Palsey, I'd have told her long ago, but now I can't, it's too late—too late," and thus making himself miserable and uneasy, Cyril entered his office to give the customary orders, and then prepared to walk to Picadilly.

Leaving Cyril, we must now follow Helen to Holburn station. The train was in as she reached the station, and she had a rush for it; but she succeeded in securing a fairly comfortable seat in a third class carriage with only three people in it besides herself.

Having made some notes in her pocket book,

she proceeded to read "Pearson's Weekly," and soon became engrossed in its contents. By the time the train stopped at Richmond, the carriage was empty, and Helen was loth to leave her comfortable seat. Seizing her umbrella, she jumped blithely on to the platform, and glanced quickly at every passenger. No, Gladys had certainly not come to meet her. Giving up her ticket, she found herself on the open platform, and ordering a cab, she got in, telling the man to drive to number 8, Down Terrace. She then lent back, determined to enjoy everything that came under her notice. " It seems a big place " she said, as she drove through the crowded High Street of Richmond, halting every now and then to let a dust cart or some other vehicle pass them.

At last the Terrace Gardens came in view and Helen knew it would not be long before the cab stopped.

She was right ; just then it stopped in front of a row of large built houses and having paid her fare Helen ran up the steps and rang the bell.

It was answered by a stout middle aged woman.

In reply to Helen's enquiry she replied in hearty tones " Oh yes miss, Miss Lincarrol is in right enough, she's been expecting you all the morning almost.

Mrs. Norton had hardly uttered her statement, when Gladys herself came flying downstairs and in a minute she had her arms round Helen's neck and was hugging and kissing her to death.

"Oh Helen," she cried "how kind of you to come so soon, you dont know what a lot I have to tell you."

"I am quite sure you have dear" answered Helen "I was delighted to be able to come with out any bother"

"Didn't Mr. Sheene mind?" enquired Gladys leading Helen up the richly carpeted stair-case." Oh not at all answered Helen brightly he seemed quite pleased for me to have a holiday, and he gave me this" she added holding up a bright gold piece.

At this juncture they arrived at Gladys's bed-room, and drawing back a red plush curtain they emerged into a dainty little bedroom furnished entirely in sea green and bamboo

"Oh! what a charming room" gasped Helen thinking of her own plain room at home compared to this perfect little paradise.

"Yes it is rather pretty" replied Gladys indifferently, all my rooms are on this landing you know!

"How many have you?" asked Helen in suprise. "My sitting room is opposite this, and there is a dear little conservatory opening out of it in which I keep all my pet plants" replied Gladys "I think that is quite enough for one girl don't you?"

"Quite" responded Helen "but where does Mr. Palsey sleep if you don't mind me asking."

"Oh James has his appartments on the floor above this" said Gladys "now do take off your hat, and come and chat in my cosy corner" and she pointed to the richly cushioned seat as she spoke.

Helen lay back in the seat and putting her hands behind her head she gazed wistfully round the room.

"Well Helen" laughed Gladys "are you longing to see my other rooms?"

"Oh no" replied Helen sadly, "this is quite lovely enough thank you, but Gladys darling do pray tell me what your parents said in the letter."

"Oh yes" said Gladys, and jumping up she opened a handsome little morocoo writing desk and took from it a sheet of writing paper closely written.

"This is it" she said sadly "I'll read it to you Helen, it makes me so miserable."

Helen listened attentively while Gladys read in a most plaintive voice the following letter:

"Speerin House
Endup Road, Norwich.
Oct. 17th.

MY DEAR GLADYS

As may be imagined your foolish letter caused both your father and I great displeasure.

We both consider your suspicions concerning James Palsey totally unfounded, and from what you say we think our niece Helen Winston must be a very foolish girl to put such notions into your head. Of course we pity her very much, as no doubt it is very sad to have one's father murdered, but to tell you the truth we think she must be a little off her head. (Violent exclamations from Helen). Referring to your letter again I see that you are determined not to Marry James. Now Gladys you must see for yourself how very nonsensical this idea is. James has every means of making you happy and what is more he is very very rich and is by no means stingy with his money, as proof the lodgings you are now in. I am sure he loves you very passionately and he is both truthful and honourable; (sarcastic smiles from both Helen and Gladys), and what is the use of forsaking this good man, whom you know and ourght to love, for some horrible scrapegrace whom you choose to consider faithful? Think over what I have said to you and try and change your mind as regards James. If you resolve to marry him your father and I are quite willing for it to take place at once; if however you persist in this obstinate behaviour, remember you are cut off from our wills and we will not have you in our house, neither will we receive any letters from you. We are not ones to encourage foolish suspicions, and are quite in favour of James. You may write again and tell us what you intend doing.

Your affectionate Mother,

Ethelreda Lincarrol.

P.S. We think the less you associate with Helen Winston the better. Your sisters and brothers are very upset and sincerely hope you will marry dear James."

" A most impertinant letter " cried Helen with burning cheeks and flaming eyes, " I had no idea my aunt was such a cruel, wicked person ; I suppose she is in league with *him*," and she pointed in the direction she thought most likely Mr. Palsey had taken.

" Oh hush Helen " said Gladys " you really have no right to speak like that ! "

" Yes I have " stormed Helen, " She dares to say I'm off my head ; it is far more likely she is off hers."

" Helen " ! cried Gladys " I really wont allow you to say such things about my mother, it is most rude of you ".

" I dont care " replied Helen " if I am to be privately insulted in this way I declare I wont stand it, I have surely had enough trouble without this—this———"

Whatever Helen intended to say she got no further, for she quite lost her self-control and burst out crying, her hot tears falling through her fingers and dropping on to her patent

leather shoes. Poor Helen ! it was indeed sad
to have all the miseries of her past life recalled
by a few thoughtless words expressed in a
letter.

Gladys who was sympathy itself, jumped up
and ran to Helen's side.

Putting her arms round her neck she kissed
her, saying as she did so " never mind Helen
dear, don't cry, I should not have hurt your
feelings so, but cheer up and I'll tell you some
news which will show you that we have *some*
friends, who are not on Mr. Palsey's side."

Helen, who quickly got over her fits of
sorrow dried her eyes and looked up.

" What is it ? " she asked.

Gladys sat down again and opening her
mother's letter said " you know what Mother
says in the post-script, about my sisters and
brothers being very upset and longing for me
to marry James ? "

" Yes " answered Helen, " but how many
have you got, I understood you were a very
small family ? "

" Oh no, we are rather a large family " responded Gladys, " perhaps I had better tell you
our names or you wont understand the news."

" Yes please do " pleaded Helen.

" Well I have three brothers and three sisters
said Gladys ", Lionel is the eldest of the family,
he's about 25 or 26 I think, then there is
Wilelmina, we always call her Minna, she is

24, then Lawrence is about 23 I fancy. I am the next, and I suppose you know I have just come of age. Ethel and Elsie (the twins) are just 19, and Hugh is the youngest, he is between 17 and 18."

"You all seem to have very fanciful names" said Helen.

"Do we?" said Gladys "well Mother is just that kind you know, her name being Ethelreda Aurora, I suppose she thinks we ought to have fancy names."

"Yes I suppose so" replied Helen, "I certainly think you have sweet names, Ethel and Elsie are very nice for twins, are they pretty?"

"Ethel and Elsie?" asked Gladys "oh yes fairly so they are both fair you know."

"You must be a fair family" replied Helen "You are fair yourself."

"Oh no we're not" answered Gladys, "Minna is like a gipsy almost and the boys are all dark."

"Really?" said Helen "well Gladys what about this wonderful piece of news"?

"Oh yes" said Gladys, "well when Mother wrote that postcript, I dont believe she asked the others about it at all, because only the other evening, I got a letter from Lawrence, (he is my favourite) and it seems he is quite in favour of me *not* marrying James."

"How lovely!" exclaimed Helen.

"I'll try and find the letter" said Gladys "it really is awfully nice, he says he never liked the look of James and he quite believes my suspicions are right and he says he'll try and find out who murdered Mr. Winston if he can, and he strongly advises me to marry Lord Beaufort, (a friend of ours who has a regard for me). He also says that he will try and come to see me, Minna is very much of his oppinion too it seems, but I think that is because *she* has her eye on James. The twins have not much to say in the matter except they think I am silly to miss such a chance, Lionel says so too, but then he is very high and mighty, you know, so of course he wants me to marry some one rich."

"Well I dont see much good in looking for the letter now you have told me all the news" said Helen laughingly, as Gladys having turned her desk up side down, was rampaging about the bookcase.

"I suppose its not much good" replied Gladys wearily," well now Helen the question I want you to settle is this ; what am I to write and tell Mother, and when am I to expect Lawrence?

"Well my dear, as regards the latter question I am quite ignorant" said Helen "your brother may turn up today for all I know."

"How jolly if he does" replied Gladys "it will be very awkward if James is at home, because if ever a man knew how to make himself disagreable James is that person."

" Is he really " ? exclaimed Helen " well I hope Lawrence will come today if that is the case, but now Gladys to business, you must write to your mother you know, and have you decided what you will say ? "

" Yes I have " said Gladys bravely " I will write at once and say that my suspicions are none the less keen, and on no plea whatever will I marry James."

" Gladys, you are good ! " cried Helen, while her friend's lips trembled and her eyes filled with tears," but never mind dear " she added " you will be well rewarded one day, when you find yourself the happy wife of a good man, he may be rich too, because it is not always the bad that are rich."

" I know " answered Gladys " and now Helen there is just time before lunch for me to write my letter."

Arranging her writing table, Gladys sat down and wrote the following letter :

8, Down Terrace.,
Richmond.
Oct. 17th.

My dearest Mother,

No words can express how sorry I am that my letter should have caused you and father so much trouble. My suspicions however have in no way diminished. James is as bad as ever. He has a horrible sneaking way of coming upstairs and he dreams too and shouts out "oh why did I do it; murder! robbery". So tonight I shall tell him that I have found him out and could not possibly marry him. Of course he will have nothing to do with me and I shall be penniless, but as *you* will have no more to say to me, I suppose I am welcome to fall back upon the kindness of my dearly beloved friend Helen Winston. Now dear Mother, as this is the last letter I shall ever write you, I beg that you will give my very best love to dear Father and all the rest, Remember me very kindly to all my friends especially Lord Beaufort. Begging heartily for your forgiveness (which I suppose you will never grant me)

   I remain, your devoted daughter
         GLADYS.

Having finished this epistle Gladys stamped and sealed it and handing it to Helen said: "You will post this on your way home wont you?"

"Oh yes" said Helen and she placed the envelope in her pocket.

"Now the next best thing to be done is, to go and see if lunch is ready exclaimed Gladys and leading the way, the two girls crossed the passage and entered a charming little drawing room. A fire burnt brightly in the grate and a table was spread in the middle of the room, on which a hot pheasant was waiting to be carved.

" Is this a drawing room or a dining room " enquired Helen, looking at the pretty pictures, the sofa and various drawing room articles.

" Both " replied Gladys " you see after meals, the flaps of this table are let down, an Indian silk cloth put upon it, and it is a sweet little table for the centre of a drawingroom,

" How dodgy " cried Helen in delight. Lunch was soon over and the girls repaired to Glady's bedroom, which was brighter and sunnier than the drawing-room. Taking their seats by the window, they both sank into silence."

Gladys was the first to break it.

" Helen " she said " when James comes home tonight, I shall tell him exactly what I think about this matter ; and if he turns me out of the house, where can I go ! "

" Dont despair " said Helen " your brother may arrive before that.

" Oh " said Gladys scornfully " its not likely ; I must say Helen you are very unsympathetic, perhaps if you were living with the prospect of spending a night with no roof over your head, you would be nicer to me "

" I am not nasty " returned Helen ; if such a thing does happen that you dont know where to go, why you can come to me, you know you will be welcome ; you see Gladys I've had so much trouble myself, that I find it easy to be calm during other peoples misery."

" Well it appears you do " replied Gladys, " but anyhow you will surely help me pack my things, for if James turns me away I shall be quite ready to start."

" Oh certainly " said Helen, and accordingly the hour and a half was spent in turning out Gladys's wardrobes etc. and by the time the trunks were locked and the room set tidy, it was nearly tea-time.

Mrs. Norton (the Landlady brought some buttered toast and tea into the bedroom, as it was more comfortable than the sitting room.

" Oh dear it has commenced to rain " cried Gladys, and walking to the window she drew back the pretty muslin curtain.

Helen followed and the two girls stood for a moment looking out of the window, through which a few rain-drops were splashing on to the Turkish carpet.

Helens eyes wandered listlessly across the terrace gardens, but she did not take in the scene before her, as she gazed intently at the lively throng before her, her thoughts were far away in the dingy little home-office, and she was wondering if Cyril would permit Gladys to dwell under his roof.

All of a sudden Gladys clutched hold of Helen's arm, and pointed to a figure in the

street, which was coming quickly up the steps
of the house.

" Oh Helen he has come ! " she cried " quick,
quick we must come down stairs ! "

The two girls rushed to the door, but ere
they had time to take a dozen steps, they were
met at the top of the stairs by *Mr. Palsey*.

Helen's cheeks and lips grew white as a
sheet, and she crept behind the welcome shade
of Gladys's back, as the gaze of the man she
hated fell upon her.

" What is the meaning of this ? " hissed Mr.
Palsey between his teeth.

" The meaning of what ? " enquired Gladys
in a trembling voice.

" This—this—most un-called-for visit ? "
cried Mr. Palsey pointing to where Helen
stood trembling like a leaf in every limb.

" It means " cried Gladys in a loud tone,
" that I know all Mr. James Palsey, all your
false deceitful ways, all your cruel treatment of
my cousin Helen and above all the murder of
her father, and the robbery of the safe ! "

Mr. Palsey grew livid with fury and fear,
and clung for support to the bannisters.

" Oh you know all that do you ? " he enquired
sardonically, " For once your imaginations have
gone too far Miss Gladys Lincarrol, I did not
murder Mr. Winston as it happens, perhaps
his daughter can throw light on that subject."

" What do you mean ? " cried Helen fiercely.

" What I say " replied Mr. Palsey.

" If you mean to infer Mr. Palsey " that
Cyrill has had anything to do with the murder
you are wrong, he is far too honourable for that."

" Of course he is " said Mr. Palsey sarcasti-
cally.

" Then dont talk about what you dont know
anything about " retorted Helen.

Mr. Palsey was about to reply, when Gladys
interupted him, " well it is of no use to prolong
matters James " she said " so I'll tell you
straight what I mean ; of course I shall not
dream of becoming your wife after what I have
discovered about you, and so I am going away ;
my parents will not have me at home, so I am
going back with Helen Winston, till my brother
Lawrence comes to fetch me, he will no doubt
set me up comfortably and then I shall at least
be free from your clutches, even if I am forced
into marrying a poor man.

Mr. Palsey turned an ashy grey and his
cruel green eyes gleamed viciously " What ? "
he gasped " you say you're going away, going
to leave the man who has never been anything
but loving to you ; I tell you, you shant do it,
you young cat— " and seizing hold of Gladys's
slender wrists he tried to force her back into
the bedroom.

Helen uttered a cry and with a blind idea of
doing some good, she flung herself across Mr.
Palsey's arms.   Seeing his chance Mr. Palsey

thrust Helen aside and tightning his grip on Gladys pinioned her to the wall, violently shaking her by the shoulders every time she opened her lips to speak.

At this critical moment, a loud ring was heard at the door quickly followed by voices in the hall below, the next moment steps were heard hastily ascending the stairs. Before anyone could speak, Mr. Palsey felt himself violently punched in the back, and Gladys recovering herself in a moment sank sobbing into the arms of *her brother*.

Lawrence Lincarrol was a tall, broad shouldered young man about 6 ft 2 inches. His hair was dark, rather curly and plentiful and was parted at the side. He had dark blue eyes a dark moustache and great regularity of features, but there was no resemblance to Gladys in his face whatever. In age, our hero was about three and twenty.

Having embraced his sister and shaken hands with Helen Lawrence turned his attention to Mr. Palsey who was shivering in the back-ground.

" Well ! " he cried, after scanning the villian from head to foot, "this is nice conduct I must say ; may I ask what you were doing with my sister when I came in ? "

"Oh I was merely advising her to keep out of draughts," replied Mr. Palsey glaring at the newcomer with hatred in his eyes.

A Crisis

"A most extraordinary way of giving your advice" replied Lawrence, "you were shaking her as if she was an animal."

"She is obstinate" persisted Mr. Palsey.

"Don't talk nonsense" cried Lawrence hotly, "a man who can contrive murders and robberies as well as you can, should be able to give a reasonable answer to a simple question, tell me at once, why were you shaking my sister in that horrible manner."

"If you think you can master me Mr. Lincarrol" said Mr. Palsey, "you will soon find your mistake, stand out of my way or we shall come to blows."

Lawrence did not move an inch, and Gladys and Helen waited with beating hearts, to see what would follow.

Mr. Palsey's evil nature was roused in a moment with a cow-like jump, and with the fury of a lion, he sprang upon Lawrence, dealing him a terrible blow between the eyes.

But in his rage Mr. Palsey had forgotten how much weaker and smaller he was than his combatant.

With wonderful coolness, Lawrence siezed Mr. Palsey by the shoulders and after a brief struggle, suceeded in forcing him backwards into the drawing room where he locked the door and slipped the key into his pocket.

"I did not wish to fight on a lodging house landing," he said turning to the girls "it might

173

get talked about, Mr. Palsey will have time to grow cool locked in there for a little, I'll let him out soon."

"Yes, dont forget" said Gladys "Mrs. Norton will think it so strange."

"Well Gladys" said Helen "I really must go now; Cyril will be expecting me, and now that your brother has come you will be quite safe."

"Oh Helen!" cried Gladys "you cant go yet, Lawrence what are we to do?"

"I was going to tell you" replied Lawrence. "Lord Beaufort is living in London now, 26 Portman Square, and as he knows I am here too, he wants me to bring you Gladys to stay with him. I shall be there for a few days longer before I go home, but I dare say you and Lord Beaufort will have arranged matters by then.

Gladys blushed hard and pretended not to hear.

"We can all go to Holburn together by the next train" proceeded Lawrence, "and then when we have seen Miss Winston safely into a cab, we can drive to Portman Sq. where Lord Beaufort will be ready to receive us."

It is very kind of you" said Helen "but I really feel very mean presuming upon you like this."

"Not at all" replied Lawrence "it is the least we could do; and now Gladys if you are ready, we ought to be starting."

" I shant be long " cried Gladys " I've only my things to put on, and my boxes to strap."

" Well then I'll just go and see about a fly " replied Lawrence, glancing at his watch as he spoke, " you be ready by the time I get back will you ? "

" Oh yes " answered Gladys, and darting back into her bedroom she commenced to put on her hat and jacket while Helen wrote labels for the luggage.

In a few moments Lawrence returned and running upstairs knocked at the bedroom door.

" Oh come in " cried Gladys " I'm nearly ready."

" Do hurry we've not so very much time " replied Lawrence, dragging out a large black trunk and carrying it to the landing where a cab man was waiting to take it down stairs.

" Now, I'm ready " said Gladys, " come on Helen."

" I am coming " replied Helen and picking up her umbrella, she followed the others downstairs.

" Oh I say we must'nt forget Mr. Palsey " cried Lawrence " I can hear him muttering in there now, I expect he is awfully wild."

" I expect he is " laughed Gladys.

Lawrence produced the key from his pocket and was about to slip it quietly into the lock, when Helen interrupted him : " Mr Lincarrol " she said " don't you think it would be safer to give the key to Mrs. Norton, because if Mr.

Palsey hears you opening the door he would be sure to get out and then there might be another scene."

"So there might" replied Lawrence, "well I think that would be the best, come along Gladys, the sooner we get off the better."

"Let me out, let me out" screamed Mr. Palsey from within the drawing room, "I'll tell the police of it; let me out this instant."

"Have patience" shouted Lawrence, but his words were hardly audible for Mr. Palsey was releiving his feelings by kicking violently at the door.

"The hall door was open, and Mrs. Norton was standing by it waiting for her lodgers to come down.

"Well miss this is short notice" she began in an injured tone.

"I am very sorry" replied Gladys "but I have to leave in a great hurry, I would have let you know before had it been possible," and she handed a few soverigns to the land lady.

"By the by Mrs. Norton" began Lawrance "here is the key of your drawing room, Mr. Palsey is in there for reasons which I dont see fit to mention now, but as I found him assaulting a lady when I arrived I shall see fit to inform the police and no doubt you will be kind enough to take charge of the key until my return."

"Oh yes sir" replied Mrs. Norton, who had no great devotion for that cross-grained Mr.

Palsey as she called him "you can trust me fully."

"Thank you" replied Lawrence, noting down Mrs. Norton's name and address in his memoranda as he spoke.

A cab drew up at the door at that moment and the landlady and parlour maid both walked down the steps with their lodgers.

"Am I to expect you back at any particular time sir?" enquired Mrs. Norton.

"I cant say for certain" answered Lawrence, "but I will probably be back some time tonight."

"Very well sir, I'll keep the key safe in my pocket till then" and Mrs. Norton slipped the key into its receptable.

"The old station" cried Lawrence and jumping into the cab he shut the door with a bang.

The journey passed off very successfully, Helen and Gladys both taking a doze in the train and waking up quite fresh at Holburn Station.

"I must go to the Police Station at once" said Lawrence "so I'll see you both started first; what is your address Miss Winston?"

"I could easily walk" replied Helen blushing, "but if you would rather I drove the address is 132, Cannon Street."

Lawrence hailed two hansoms "now Gladys jump in as you have further to go" he said,

" 26, Portman Square " he added to the cabman, who touched his hat and drove off in an
instant.

The second hansom was waiting and drew
close up to the curb as the other drove off.
" 132, Cannon Street, shouted Lawrence,
" goodbye Miss Winston, be sure and write to
Gladys if you are in trouble, I am going there
myself late tonight as unfortunately I must go
back to Richmond to see about Mr. Palsey."

" Thank you very very much " replied Helen
the tears gathering in her pretty eyes as she
spoke. But she soon wiped them away and
leaning back in the comfortable hansom she
commenced to hum a little tune as she arranged
her ruffled hair at the little looking glass.
Little did she dream how very soon she would
have to avail herself of Lawrence's offer.

A dismal sleet had begun to fall and being
tired Helen was not sorry when the hansom
stopped at the dreary looking office. Lawrence
had already paid the man so Helen had only
to collect her parcels and get out.

A light was shining in the office room and
also in Cyril's bedroom which was just above it.

" How very strange " thought Helen as she
mounted the steps. Before she had time to
lay her hand on the bell the door was violently
opened from within and there stood Netherby,
looking very pale and trembling from head to
foot.

178

"Oh come in Miss, do come in" he cried in an agitated voice as Helen stood staring at his strange appearance.

"Why Netherby, what *is* the matter?" cried Helen entering the passage and closing the door behind her.

"Oh dont ask me Miss, please dont let me be the first to tell you" cried Netherby and the poor man clung for support to the door handle.

"Very well, dont distress yourself" said Helen kindly and calmly and seeing there was no more information to be got from him, she entered the office.

It seemed to be in a state of utter confusion; papers littered the whole room, Cyril's tea stood untouched by his desk, and Cyril's own private chest was wide open and Wilson the other clerk was cooly reading the papers and documents within. He glanced over his shoulder as Helen entered and with an insolent grin returned to the parchment in his hand.

All Helen's pride and dignity was roused in a moment.

"Wilson!" she cried with an impatient movement of her hands, but keeping perfectly cool the while "oblige me by telling me the meaning of this conduct."

"The explanation is there" replied the clerk pointing to a half sheet of paper lying on the desk.

It was a common bit of ruled paper and by the ragged edge had evidently been hastily torn from a note book ; a pin was run through the top of the paper showing it had been attached to something.

"Where did you find this" enquired Helen before reading it.

"We found it pinned to Mr. Sheene's desk addressed to you miss," replied Netherby who had entered the room, "it was Mrs. Marshland who told us to open it.

"Very well" said Helen, and she read as follows.

"Darling. When you see this I shall probably be miles away. This is written to bid you goodbye as it is not likely we shall meet again. When you read my story try and forgive me ; for in spite of all I always loved you and ever will.

CYRIL SHEENE.

This strange epistle was hastily scrawled in pencil and the signature was very shaky, but Helen knew the writing in a minute, it was undoubtedly Cyril's.

"It is not likely that we shall meet again ! !"

The words ran through Helen's bewildered head and repeated themselves again and again. Cyril, whom she had loved so dearly and believed in so faithfully had gone away, left her alone in the cruel heartless world ; Cyril

whom she had never even had course or reason
to call dishonourable had written himself to
ask her to try and forgive him. What did it
mean? And the story, where was the story?"
The room seemed to swim round; " we shall
not meet again, try and forgive me" The
story where is the story? And then all was in
darkness and Helen remembered no more.

CHAPTER XXV

A REMOVAL TO PORTMAN SQUARE

When Helen recovered she found herself lying
in a large comfortable bed propped up with
pillows. The room was large, cheerful and
beautifully furnished. A small table covered
with a white cloth was by the bedside with
medicine bottles upon it. A bright fire burnt
in the grate. The blinds were down and warm
red curtains were pulled across the large bow
window.

A small lamp was carefully placed where no
light or glare could reach the bed and the
very atmosphere of the room spoke of extreme
comfort.

A nurse, in a white cap and apron was
gliding noiselessly about the room arranging
things here and there.

For a moment Helen lay quite still staring
about her plerpexedly, but on making a slight

movement in the bed the nurse turned round, "So you are awake at last miss?" she said in a slow gentle voice, "do you know you have slept quite quietly for three hours."

"Where are am I?" asked Helen gazing from the kind face of the nurse around the strange room.

"You are in Lord Beaufort's house in Portman Square" replied the nurse.

"Lord Beaufort?" repeated Helen, "I have heard the name before."

"Yes you have" said the nurse, "Miss Lincarrol is here you know, and her brother, and your old servant Mrs. Marshland, so you see no one has deserted you."

"Except Cyril" sighed Helen.

"You must not think of that now" replied the nurse soothingly, "all you have to do is rest and keep quiet; I expect Miss Lincarrol will be up soon, she has come twice already only you were asleep, now take your medicine and then lay quiet; you will hear all the story soon from other lips than mine."

Thus reassured Helen took her cooling draught and lay down, patiently awaiting any visitor who would enlighten her as to past events. Her thoughts naturally enough wandered back to the episode of Cyril's departure and she was getting extremely restless, much to the nurse's dismay, when the door softly opened and Gladys appeared in the room.

With a smile she instantly ran to the bedside and Helen tried to raise herself to greet her friend, but her head instantly swam round and she fell back on the pillow, white and gasping. The nurse gave her a dose of medicine and she quickly came to herself again.

"You must not try to exert yourself too much" said the nurse kindly, "it will do you no good, and will only hinder your recovery."

"Very well" said Helen faintly, "but how is it I get so queer?"

"Because your head is in a weak state" replied the nurse, "and it will probably injure you very much to rampage."

It would take too long to relate the history of Helen's illness as Helen heard it from Gladys lips, with all the details and exagertions, so we will go back a little bit and see what happened after Helen swooned away.

CHAPTER XXVI

THE CONTENTS OF THE CHEST

As soon as Netherby (the clerk) saw what had happened he at once called for Marshland, who was sitting in the parlour in a state of utter collapse. On hearing that her precious Miss Helen had fainted, the good old woman ran at once to the office room.

Helen lay perfectly white and still upon the floor with Cyril's fatal letter clenched in her hand. Marshland instantly knelt down and placed her head at Helen's heart. " She is not dead " she cried triumphantly.

" What can we do ? " asked Netherby in a shaky voice.

" I'll tell you " said Marshland getting up off the floor, you must take a cab and drive as fast as you can to Portland Square number 26, Miss Lincarrol is staying there with Lord Beaufort and I think her brother too ; they are all staunch friends of Miss Helen's I know they will come at once, we can make no move, friendless as we are, without the help of Mr. Lincarrol or some one ".

" Stop a bit " cried Netherby regaining his courage all of a sudden ; something tells me the story Mr. Sheene speaks of in his letter is somewhere in the private chest, and as it is evidently meant for Miss Winston's private reading, I'll trouble you Mr. Wilson to let those papers alone and give me up the key."

" What right have you to the key any more than me ? " asked Wilson suddenly.

" None I suppose " replied Netherby " but I know that you are subjecting yourself to the penalty of the law by ransacking that private chest, I shall inform the police if you don't instantly deliver the key."

Netherby's altered manner rather cowed Wilson so very sulkily he gave up the key.

Then with a set determination Netherby collected all the papers etc : which Wilson had strewn over the desks tying them firmly together placed them back in the chest.

"Have you any more?" asked he before locking the chest.

"No" stoutly declared Mr. Wilson.

"I'm not so eager to belive you" replied Netherby.

"Why not?" enquired Wilson savagely.

"Because you're not extra fond of the truth" replied Netherby "and I'd rather satisfy myself that you have no more papers about you before I lock the chest."

"You'd better dare lay a finger on me" hissed Wilson.

"I dont want to" replied Netherby "but if you really have taken nothing, what is your objection to letting me see the contents of your pocket?"

"Oh I'll let you see the contents drawled Wilson and he proceeded to place a few articles on the desk.

Netherby was beginning to satisfy himself it was alright, when he noticed Wilson shuffling about with the inner pocket of his coat.

"Hurry up" exclaimed Netherby impatiently.

"Alright" cried Wilson nervously drawing

out a rather dirty handkerchief; but fate was against him and with the handkerchief came a roll of bank notes.

Marshland gave a cry as she beheld the sight of the unhappy Wilson slink into a corner.

Netherby collected the notes placed them in the desk and without a word put on his hat and went out. In less than five minutes he returned accompanied by two policemen, who on a sign from Netherby advanced to Wilson and before the astonished man could say a word he found himself handcuffed and carefully guarded by two officials.

Netherby and Marshland then gave an exact account of what had taken place and Netherby ended by saying " you see Wilson if you had shut the chest when I told you and concealed nothing I should have been the last to call the police, but when it came to robbing the chest in justice to Miss Winston I had to do my duty."

Wilson was too utterly dazed to say a word, and in a few moments Netherby, not liking to leave the house sent a messenger to portman Square.

In a couple of hours a cab drew up at the door, and out got Lawrence Lincarrol, Lord Beaufort, and a short thin man, who turned out to be Cyril Sheene's solicitor.

On hearing the story, Lord Beaufort said that Helen was to be taken at once to his house and that Marshland should accompany her. Accordingly the unconcious girl was lifted into the brougham and accompanied by the old servant drove off. "Your things shall be sent on" said Lord Beaufort to Marshland as he helped her into the cab "and a trained nurse shall be got for Miss Winston, meanwhile my servants quite understand what is to be done."

Then the cab drove off and Lord Beaufort entered the office.

Lawrence and Mr. Spriggs (the solicitor) were both busy interviewing Netherby, who now that he had done his duty and shown much good sence had relapsed into his old nervous state.

We had here better describe Lord Beaufort and Mr. Spriggs.

Lord Beaufort was a half Spaniard, his mother being of that nationality and his father (who was dead) an Englishman.

He took after his mother in looks. He was moderately tall and thin and might have been eighty and thirty. He had straight black hair and beard and moustache, to match, the former being small and well cut, not the bushy kind. His handsome dark eyes were quite those of a foreigner and his teeth were beautifully white. He was particulally well dressed and even to his boots.

Very different indeed was Mr. Spriggs. A

thin wiry little man about 5 feet 2 inches, with thin sandy coloured hair (a trifle bald), twinkly little blue eyes, a very pink face and carroty coloured moustache. He was attired in a rough tweed suit with knickaboccers, a turn down collar, very untidily put on, thick grey stockings, clumping boots, a green tie, and a dear stalker cap drawn well on to his head.

"Well the first thing to be done" said Mr. Spriggs in jerky tones "is to open the chest, and I being the solicitor will proceed to do it," and he stalked accross the room with a very high and mighty air and made a great commotion with the keys.

The chest being opened the contents were carefully examined. A blue envelope was first opened and contained the following information.

"This is to say that I, Cyril Sheene leave all my money, which is all in bank notes to my intended Helen Winston ; it is not very much and does not exceed £150 but still I hope it will do as I can't afford any more. Dated August 11th.

This was all written in violet coloured ink by Cyril himself ; but at the bottom of the paper a few lines were hastily scrawled in pencil.

"I hereby add that all my share of the money I stole from Mr. John Winston is in

the black leather bag at the back of the chest.
Helen will recognise the bag. Not a farthing
has been spent and it is all to go to Helen.
Dated October 14

"That was written on the day of Mr.
Sheene's departure announced Mr. Spriggs as
he replaced the paper in its envelope, and this
is the bag I suppose," he added dragging at a
black leather bundle in a remote corner of the
chest.

The bag it certainly was and on being
opened £100 in ready gold tumbled on to the
desk, and with it a slip of paper on which the
reader will remember John Winston had
written, "all this gold is bequeathed to my
daughter Helen on the day when I shall be
called upon to die," and was sealed with the
writer's prifate seal.

Nothing else of great importance appeared
except a bundle of white manuscript carefully
tied up and sealed, addressed to Helen and
marked "private".

"I know what that is!" cried Netherby
excitedly "it is the story Mr. Sheene wrote
about, look here sir" and he picked up Cyril's
letter which had dropped from Helen's hand
when she was lifted into the cab.

Mr. Spriggs carefully read the letter and
placed it in the chest, "ah yes" he said addressing Lord Beaufort and Lawrence, "that story

is evidently for Miss Winston's private eye, so it must be locked up till she is able to read it."

"Which wont be for a good while judging from her present condition," said Lawrence, "but now to business, what about this office, it is a difficult matter to carry it on without Mr. Sheene."

"As far as I can see, it must be kept on till Miss Winston's recovery" replied Mr. Spriggs "if no more news is heard of Mr. Sheene till then well Miss Winston can come and procure her money and various other papers which will of course be hers and then this place can be sold."

"Yes" said Lord Beaufort and I suppose Mr. Netherby will be the head man till then.

"Well yes" replied Mr. Spriggs "he must certainly be here to look after the place, and of course I shall look in occasionally to see all goes well; another young man can be got to be under Mr. Netherby as Mr. Wilson has gone to prison for attempted robbery; do you agree to that Mr. Netherby?"

"Oh yes sir" eagerly replied the clerk, who would not have disagreed for the world.

"And if it comes to the place being sold" added Lord Beaufort "you can come to me Mr. Netherby, I may have arranged something by then"

"Thank you very much sir" replied Netherby and after a few more matters had been arranged the three men left the office leaving Netherby in charge.

By the time Lord Beaufort and Lawrence got back home, a doctor had seen Helen. He said that when she recovered her senses, perfect rest and quiet would be all she needed, her brain being in a dazed condition. She would not be able to leave her bed for some time probably though nothing serious was the matter.

Helen remained unconcious all night and next day she was very delirious but towards 4 o'clock she dropped asleep and woke up about seven o'clock, her right senses returned to her, but still in a weak condition.

CHAPTER XXVII

THE PROPOSAL

It was not untill the evening after Helen's recovery that Lawrence and Lord Beaufort had an oppertunity of conversing together.

Mulberry Beaufort was seated in his luxurious study partaking of some Burgundy wine and reading a detective story, when the door opened and Lawrence, entered, tired after a long day in the city.

"Well Mulberry" he said throwing himself down in an arm chair and lighting a cigar, " no news of Sheene in the Star I suppose?"

"Not a word" replied Mulberry, "it is a most misterious affair altogether."

"Yes the odd part of it is that Palsey has made off too" answered Lawrence.

"You dont mean that!" cried Mulberry.

"Yes I do" said Lawrence, "it appears the villain got off while I was away; you know I locked him in the drawing room and as the landlady had the key he would not have made his exit in that way.

"No" replied Mulberry "he certainly could not but you forget the window."

"No I dont" responded Lawrence, "that is just where he did get out, for when I opened the door of the drawing room, the window was wide open at the bottom, and a bit of rope was fastenned to a hook on the window ledge and hanging out of the window, so the wreatch made his escape that way; it is a wonder he was not detected for the police are every where on the look out for him and I am sure if ever a man deserved the gallows he does."

"Yes indeed" replied Mulberry lazily puffing at his cigar "but in my opinion the disappearance of Sheene is the most extraordinary it was so very sudden and unexpected, whereas it was not at all an unlikely thing for Palsey to do, seeing he was so angry at being locked in."

"My idea is" answered Lawrence "that they both had their own reasons for wishing to leave so abruptly. I shouldnt be at all supprised if the villian Palsey knowing the police were on his track, dropped some hint as to Sheene's share in the murder and so got the blame partly shifted from himself."

"Then you think Sheene did share in the murder do you"? asked Mulberry, his black eyes flashing.

"I do" replied Lawrence, "I bet you a shilling that story of Sheene's will reveal everything. It strikes me Sheene made off on account of the police too"—

"Well I only hope Miss Winston will soon be well enough to read the story" replied Mulberry.

"I hope so too" responded Lawrence heartily.

"I suppose Netherby still stays at the office"? enquired Mulberry.

"Oh yes" answered Lawrence, "but it will be a good thing for him as soon as he can leave, he gets very little pay and he is really a very good fellow indeed".

"Yes he is" rejoined Mulberry "I will try and get something for him as soon as possible."

Just then the door opened and in came Gladys looking very pretty in her evening dress of rose coloured silk.

She blushed on seeing the two men, but came forward gracefully enough.

"I came to see if you were coming into the drawing room" she said "dinner will soon be ready and I have just been to see Helen".

" Oh how is she " ? asked Lawrence.

" Better I think " replied Gladys " I am going up again after dinner."

" Well I will come to the drawing room " said Mulberry putting aside his tumbler.

" Will you come too Lawrence ? "

"Not yet thanks " replied Lawrence " I have a letter to write, I will join you at dinner "

" We expect a few guests tonight" said Mulberry.

" Oh very weil" said Lawrence " I'll change presently."

Mulberry opened the door and he and Gladys betook themselves from the study.

Alone in the beautiful drawing room with the light from the tall standing lamp falling on her fair features, Mulberry Beaufort became entranced with Gladys's beauty.

He stood gazing into her lovely blue eyes with his own black ones, till he could contain himself no longer.

" Gladys darling " he exclaimed passionately seizing her small white hand " I love you."

Gladys blushed and tried to hide her face but Mulberry caught her other hand and kept his eyes full on her."

" Answer me Gladys " cried the lover " I love you so much and if you will only be my wife my happiness will be complete."

"Oh Lord Beaufort" cried Gladys " this is so unexpected ".

"Call me Mulberry"! he almost whispered.

"Well Mulberry" murmured Gladys "I really dont know what to say."

"Think darling" cried Mulberry, "surely you dont wish to crush all hope and happiness out of my life, my heart beats only for you Gladys, you dont wish to stop it do you"?

"Oh no" earnestly replied Gladys.

"Then may I take that as your acceptation of me"? enquired Mulberry.

"I think you may" replied Gladys softly.

Mulberry was too overpowered with joy to say a word, he merely clasped her in his arms and drew her head on to his shoulder, where it lay in a state of bliss for the space of three minutes.

At length she slowly raised it and Mulberry taking one of her hands pressed it tight saying, "then darling, we may consider ourselves engaged"?

"Yes Mulberry!" murmered Gladys.

"Then dear accept this as a token" said Mulberry and as he spoke he slipped a handsome diamond and saphire ring on her finger.

She had scarcely recovered her astonishment and pleasure when the butler entered announcing Mr. and Mrs. Vermont.

CHAPTER XXVIII

THE DINNER PARTY

THE Hon : Mr. and Mrs. Vermont were only the first of great numbers who flocked to Lord Beaufort's house that evening. By the time the dinner gong sounded the large drawing room was filled with ladies and gentlemen many of whom had brought instruments to play, as Mulberry intended it to be a musical evening.

Mulberry eyed Gladys lovingly as he gave his arm to Mrs. Murry and escorted her to the dining room.

The dinner table was a sight to behold!

Pink was the colour chosen for the evening.

The daintily arranged menus were set in white porcelain frames on which pink roses were beautifully painted. In the centre of the table stood a valuable vase in which large pink roses were arranged. The numerous wax candles were covered with pink shades, and among the ferns and plants which adorned the room hung little pink electric lights ; and everything that could be was ornemented with pink satin ribbon and bunches of roses.

It may here be said that owing to Helen's illness Lord Beaufort had not had late dinner so the sight was quite new to Gladys.

Three footmen with powdered hair and chocolate and drab livery were in attendance.

"Oh Mulberry what is this"? asked Gladys,

pointing to one of the beautifully decorated menus.

"Oh that is the menu of my table d'hote" replied Mulberry carelessly, "this is of nightly recurrence".

"How delightful"! cried Gladys and sitting down she carefully studied the menu which was as follows :

MENU DU DINER.

Wednesday, October 20th

Hors d'œuvres.
Consommé Parsanne.
Crême d'asperges.
Sole normande.
Selle de mouton à l'anglaise.
Jambon de York à la Zingara.
Pommes maitre d'hôtel.
Poularde à la broche.
Salade de saison.
Glace marigan.
or
Gateaux Mignons.
Fromage.
Dessert.

THE SECOND ENTRÉE MAY BE EXCHANGED FOR MACARONI.

As can be imagined the dinner took a good time, but when at length it drew to a close the company proceeded to the drawing room where they settled down for some good music.   Mr.

Vermont was the first to contribute to the
entertainment. He played "Intermezzo" as
a solo violin, and the beautiful melody only
added to both Mulberry's and Gladys's happiness. Many others also played and sang,
and at last by dint of great persuasion Gladys
consented to sing. She had a magnificent
clear soprano voice and as he listened Mulberry
Beaufort fairly trembled for joy.

In the midst of the proceedings the dowegar
Lady Beaufort entered (Mulberry's mother).
She looked a great deal older than she was but
was still very handsome.

Her hair was silvery white, but her eyes and
complexion were very dark, and she very much
resembled her son. She was attired entirely
in black silk and white lace.

The reader may think it strange that Lady
Beaufort did not make her appearance at the
table d'hote but to tell the truth she considered
herself rather too old for such things, her age
being 75. She generally partook of a plate of
fricassed ham and a glass of sherry, by her
own fireside, but the last two nights she had
partaken of her meal with Helen.

During her repast she usually read House-
hold Hints and then on coming into the drawing room she had plenty to talk about. She
had given her son a great deal of hints as to
how he should propose and now hearing that
he was accepted she made her way to where

Gladys was sitting and proceeded to give her
some advice as to her future housekeeping.
It rather bored Gladys but being so very high
in Lady Beauforts estimation, she tried her
best to look interested.

At about 10.30, Lady Beaufort got up and
played God save the queen on the piano and
several of the guests joined in the chorus on
their violins and harps, soon after which, the
people began to depart.

"Shall you have guests tomorrow night
Mulberry?" enquired Gladys as soon as the
last visitor had strayed from the drawing room.

"No dear I don't think so, they tire me if I
have them every night" replied Mulberry.

"But you'll have the dinner I suppose?"
eagerly asked Gladys.

"Of course" replied Mulberry with a shrug
of the shoulders "as I told you Gladys it is
a nightly performance here."

"How nice!" gasped Gladys "well now
Mulberry dear I will go and see how Helen is;
shall I say good night now?"

"If it pleases you dear" answered Mulberry.

Gladys kissed him fondly and then turned to
Lady Beaufort who accompanied her upstairs.

Lawrence and Mulberry then retired to the
study for another glass of burgandy before
going to bed.

CHAPTER XXIX

THE DAWN OF LOVE

SOME few weeks had elapsed since the afore-said dinner party took place and day by day Helen grew stronger, till at length Dr. Durham pronounced her to be well enough to get up ; in fact he went so far as to say that a drive in the fresh air would do her good. As may be imagined it was a happy day for everybody, when Helen attired in her new winter clothes made her appearance in the large hall, ready for her first drive in the open air since her illness commenced.

Gladys was also there and the nurse whom Mulberry had thought it advisable to keep a little longer.

It was a nice bright day such as is seldom seen in the month of November. The victoria stood at the door and the two beautifully groomed bay horses were pauing the ground, eager to be off. Mulberry and Lawrence saw them safely off and then as they turned into the study Mulberry said " I think if Miss Winston is well enough, it would be a good thing to drive to Cannon Street this afternoon and see about reading that story of Sheenes ".

" I think so too " replied Lawrence.

Neither of the men seemed at all inclined to settle down and after wandering about a good deal, Mulberry threw himself down in a chair and gave a yawn. There was silence for a little while and at last Lawrence un-expectedly broke it by saying " I say Mulberry how long is it since you and Gladys Lincarrol have been engaged "?

Mulberry turned a dull red and began to light his pipe. " Why do you want to know "? he stammered at last.

" I'll tell you presently " replied Lawrence with a smile.

" Well I think it is about three or four weeks " answered Mulberry shuffling about from one leg to the other.

" Is that all "? enquired Lawrence.

" Yes " replied Mulberry, " now tell me why you wanted to know.

It was now Lawrence's turn to grow em-barresed, " well the truth is " he said at length " I am thinking of proposing to Helen Winston, and as I have had no experiance I would like a few hints as to how I should go ".

Mulberry laughed " well you should go to my mother for hints " he replied " she helped me very much during my little romance ".

" Well I am afraid it would hardly do for me to go up and ask Lady Beaufort to give me some hints, as I am about to propose " replied Lawrence " she would be very much taken aback I should think ".

" Not she " answered Mulberry with a shrug

of his shoulders " she would take it quite as a matter of course ; but still if you dont care to ask her, why not scribble her a note describing your position and I'll send one of the maids up with it ; why she would write you pages of advice ".

" I dont want as much as all that " cried Lawrence " I want just a few gentle hints as to how to be loving and look as if I was in earnest ".

" Well why not write to my mother " ? again repeated Mulbery.

" It will look so silly " said Lawrence " and yet I'm hard up for advice and *you* dont seem inclined to give me any "

" No, because you'd get it much better and more original from my mother " replied Mulberry.

" Well then I'll risk writing " said Lawrence getting up as he spoke " but mind if Lady Beaufort is annoyed you must take the consequences because I should never have dreamt of doing this without you ".

" Oh I'll answer for the consequences " said Mulberry with an amused smile as his friend sat down and taking a sheet of crested note paper proceeded to pen the following lines :

LADY BEAUFORT

  I hope you will excuse the liberty I take in writing you these few words—but speaking honestly I am in the very same difficulty as your son was a little time ago and out of which you so cleaverly helped him. Would it be asking too much of you to do the same for me. I am about to propose to Helen Winston and dont quite know how to express myself. I want it to be quite a short proposal and one quickly got through. Do you advise me to do it out of doors or in. I am afraid I should get so nervous in a drawing room, but of course it is just as you think best. Might I have an answer to this as soon as possible please.

   Believe me,
    Yours faithfully,
     Lawrence E. G. Lincarrol.

" Here now if Lady Beaufort turns that to ridicule its not my fault cried Lawrence hastily screwing his epistle into a cocked hat.

"No of course not" replied Mulberry encouragingly ringing the bell as he spoke, " now when the butler comes I'll tell him to send it up at once and mark my words Lawrence you'll have a reply within three minutes from now."

"I feel an awful ass" responded Laurence throwing the note on the table " but now I'm going out for a bit perhaps as you say I shall find an answer waiting for me when I come back."

"No doubt of it" said Mulberry and with that Lawrence disappeared into the hall.

The day was beautifully fine as I said before so Lawrence walked further than he had at first meant to and coming back he met Helen, Gladys and Mrs. Chizzle the nurse and at Helen's request he got into the carriage and made one of the party home.

Helen looked quite her old self again. The same bright red colour was on her cheeks and the old light in her eyes.

" I think the drive has done you good Miss Winston" remarked Lawrence noting the change in her face.

"Yes, I feel so much better" answered Helen " we drove all round Hyde Park and the air is really lovely for London."

" It is " replied Lawrence and then turning to the nurse he added "I should think you are pleased with the progress your patient is making."

" Yes " assented Mrs. Chizzle " I am."

" Do you think Miss Winston, you are well enough to drive to Cannon Street this afternoon and read Mr. Sheene's " story" ? enquired Lawrence.

" Perfectly " replied Helen with a smile.

Lawrence was astounded, " you must be prepared for bad news " he said.

" I am already prepared " said Helen.

" For the very worst ? " queried Lawrence.

" For anything " returned Helen

" That's alright then " replied Lawrence.

" Mulberry and I are going to tea with the Vermonts this afternoon, but we need not start till 4 o'clock " said Gladys.

" It would'nt matter if you were a little late " answered Lawrence.

Just then the victoria stopped and after having helped the ladies to alight, Lawrence went quickly to the study where as Lord Beaufort had predicted an envelope lay waiting to be opened addressed to Lawrence in the dowegor lady Beaufort's hand writing.

Lawrence blushed as he took up the bulky package and retired with it to the privacy of his own bedroom, where we will leave him to read it in silence.

A copy of the letter is given below :

Nov. 4th, 18—

Dear Mr. Lincarrol

It is with great pleasure that I comply with your wishes. It is not the first time I have been appealed to under such circumstances. There is an art in proposing as well as in every thing. If you are liable to nervousness, do not propose indoors. There is a very nice little nook in the back garden by the crocus bed, where my own romance took place. It is quite unfrequented from 11 to 1 and from 3 to 6.

Be careful not to be too sudden or you will make the girl shy, but do it by degrees. Keep as close to her as you can after she has accepted (which if you manage it with tact she is sure to do) draw her to you and murmer soft words.

If you wish for more details do not hesitate to write to me. Wishing you every success.

I remain
Yours etc.
Cristina Beaufort.

Lawrence folded the above and carefully put it in his blotting pad, and then with a sigh of relief he brushed his hair and went down to lunch.

CHAPTER XXX

Helen was pronounced quite well enough to drive to the office that afternoon; so accordingly the victoria was again brought to the front door and Helen, Lawrence and Mulberry all got in. It was not considered necessary for Gladys to go too.

On arriving at Cannon Street Netherby opened the door of the office, for he expected them all the morning. Mr. Spriggs (the solicitor) was there too.

Helen was soon seated at the desk and the roll of paper, containing Cyril's story was untied amidst a breathless silence.

It was very touchingly written and stated

206

Chapter XXX

how Cyril, led away by Mr. Palsey, had contrived to find out where Mr. Winston kept his money ; and how, still under Mr. Palsey's influence he had gone up to Warwick to plan the murder of poor John Winston. He fully acknowledged his guilt, but declared over and over again that he never would have done it without Mr. Palsey's aid. It ended by a heartfelt intreaty for forgiveness.

Helen's voice faltered a little in places, but she never really broke down till the last word had fallen from her lips, then she sobbed softly, while Mr. Spriggs bustled about and put away the papers.

Lawrence took Helen's hand and tried to comfort her but it seemed useless.

Meanwhile Lord Beaufort sought out Netherby and engaged him as footman. The poor man was highly delighted for he was getting no pay at present and as every one knew Mulbery Beaufort was not at all scanty in the way of wages.

Helen seemed very dull and depressed all the way home but she shed no more tears.

Soon after 5 o'clock Lawrence began to grow very restless so lighting a cigarette he strolled into the garden to enjoy the last glimpse of day-light. Some how his steps let him to the crocus bed and here he continued to walk up and down his thoughts occupied with Helen Winston.

As Lady Beaufort had said the crocus bed was a delightfully quiet spot. Not a soul was to be seen any where, and a general air of peace pervaded the whole atmosphere. Lawrence continued to walk up and down lost in his rapturous reveries, while the evening grew darker and darker. By and by the stars began to come out and at length the moon rose full in the heavens, and then Lawrence looked up and there in front of him stood Helen, clad in her evening dress of pale yellow and a white shawl thrown round her shoulders.

She seemed as supprised as Lawrence for she stopped suddenly on seeing him.

" I beg your pardon Mr. Lincarrol " she began " I hope I am not disturbing you, but Lady Beaufort told me to come here before dinner and see if Jefferson (the gardiner) had raked the beds properly ".

Lawrence grew very red and glanced quickly and mechanically up to the window of Lady Beaufort's budoir. There sure enough the old lady was looking out, but on seeing the two together she quickly retired into the regions of her own bedroom.

" This is Lady Beaufort's doing thought Lawrence as the letter he had received came back to his mind. "Oh no you dont disturb me at all " he added aloud.

Helen smiled and began plucking at the faded leaves of the trees.

Chapter XXX

"What a lovely night it is" said Lawrence at last as the silence grew embarresing.

"Yes" replied Helen vaguely and Lawrence glancing at her saw by the moonlight that her eyes had a far away dreamy look in them.

"How delightfully sheltered this part of the garden is" continued Lawrence.

"Yes very answered Helen, drawing her silk shawl over her shoulders as a slight breeze blew across the garden.

"Had you a good garden where you lived before?" enquired Lawrence, unconsiously leading up to his proposal.

"At Cannon Street there was only a yard replied Helen, a painful blush mounting to her face, "but at Kenelham we had a sweet little garden, my poor dear father took the greatest interest in his flowers and so did I" she added with a slight catch in her harmonious voice.

"Dont you now?" asked Lawrence.

"Oh yes" said Helen, "but you see, it is all so different now; in those days my father and I were constant companions and our opinions were one. But now there is nobody —nobody" and tears began to well up in her eyes and fall over her long black lashes.

"Surely somebody cares for you Miss Winston, surely there is someone to sympathise with you" interupted Lawrence.

"Oh Mr. Lincarrol you dont understand" cried Helen with a sob.

" I think I do " replied Lawrence gently, coming a little closer and taking her trembling hand. I think I understand your feelings, it must be very sad to be so—so lonely."

" Wait till your turn comes Mr. Lincarrol and you will know then " replied Helen.

" Would it be different, to have some one to care for you, to love you as your father did ? " asked Lawrence.

" Oh it would, it would " cried Helen rapturesly clasping her hands together.

" suppose some one loved you now as much if not more than your father, what would you say ? " asked Lawrence.

" I could not belive it " replied Helen promptly " unless " unless " she added, " I knew the person very well and was quite posative of the love, and had good proofs of it."

" Have you not proofs enough " ? asked Lawrence.

" Of what " ? asked Helen.

" Of my love for you " replied Lawrence.

" Your love ! ? " gasped Helen.

" Yes " repeated Laurence passionately, " oh Helen I can no longer restrain my feelings, I love you as I never before loved anyone, can I hope, can I dare to hope that you return my love " ?

Helen did not answer. She was thinking of another proposal some months past, so very unlike this one, far away on the Kenelham hill

tops, and she remembered how she had acted
then. Once more, she felt the soft sea breeze
fan her face, she saw the hills and the distant
sea and she saw oh how plainly Cyrils form by
her side, she heard his words and her own
replies, she saw his blue eyes looking so intently
at her ; and then awaking to the present she
saw another pair of blue eyes looking at her,
speaking so much more fervently than the
others and she felt the clasp of a strong hand
on her own and then raising her head she
looked at Lawrence and softly whispered
"yes".

"Oh Helen" cried Lawrence "you make
me so happy, so very happy !

Tears of joy dimmed Helen's eyes and
Lawrence taking her hand drew her head on
to his breast and told her gently of his great
love for her and how happy they both would
be. And Helen listenned feeling the happiness
had already begun.

A gentle breeze began to stir the trees and
fan the brows of the lovers as they slowly
walked along the paths of love, and the moon
looking down from her home in the heavens,
smiled on the pair and wished them joy.

CHAPTER XXXI

PREPARATIONS

As the time drew on Lord Beaufort began to make preparations for his marriage with Gladys.

He had at first thought it would be nice if Lawrence and Helen could be married on the same day, but that was found to be quite impossible as Lawrence wished to visit his home first, he had also plenty of other things to attend to before he could be married.

One evening about 10 o'clock, Gladys was seated in her bedroom enjoying a few minutes quiet before going to bed.

Her maid had already done her hair and she had changed her evening dress for a warm and comfortable dressing gown. Her room presented rather an untidy appearance as the dress maker had been there that day to bring her wedding dress which now lies in a snowy pile at the foot of the bed.

As Gladys sat still by the fire a knock sounded at the door. Before she could reply the door opened and Helen came in.

" Well Gladys, you seem to be enjoying yourself here all alone " she cried drawing her chair to the fire beside her friend.

" I was only thinking " replied Gladys with a laugh.

" Of tomorrow I suppose " put in Helen.

"Well to tell the truth I was" answered Gladys with a faint sigh.

"Well you shouldn't sigh" said Helen "only think Gladys, this time tomorrow you will be Lady Beaufort."

"I know that" said Gladys rather crossly.

"How sad you seem" said Helen in supprise.

"Do I?" enquired Gladys "well perhaps you'll feel the same the night before your marriage."

"I hope not" answered Helen promptly "Oh Gladys" she added quickly "you never told me where you are going for your honeymoon."

"How silly of me" replied Gladys cheering up "well we are going on the continent, Mulberry wishes to visit some relations of his in Venice and then I shall get him to spend a week or so in Naples, Rome, Paris and other places"

"How lovely"! cried Helen "I do envy you."

"Well wont you do the same at your honeymoon"? asked G.

"No" said Helen "Lawrence and I are going to spend a quiet fortnight at Ryde in the Isle of Wight".

"Oh I see" said Gladys.

"What time does the important ceremony take place tomorrow" demanded Helen.

"At 11 o'clock precisely" rejoined Gladys,

213

who possessed the virtue of punctuality, " at St. Pauls ".

" I see " said Helen " and when do you start on your honeymoon ? "

" We cross the channel tomorrow night " replied Gladys.

" And Lawrence and I are going to Norfolk " replied Helen.

" Are you really " ? asked Gladys.

" Yes Lawrence lives there you know " said Helen " so he thought it would be nice for me to go and see his people ; why what am I telling you this for when Lawrence is your own brother ? "

" I dont know I'm sure " laughed Gladys, " by the by Helen did Lawrence tell you that mother and father have quite softened, and are quite willing I should marry Mulberry, but they cant bring themselves to come up tomorrow to the marriage ; Lionel and Minna are coming though, so I expect they will go back to Norfolk with you and Lawrence."

" I knew all that " replied Helen " I am really quite excited about it."

" Oh Helen you must see my wedding dress" cried Gladys, and getting up the two girls walked to the bed whereon lay a flimsy mass of tule and satin crowned with orange blossom and glittering with diamonds."

" It is really a beautiful dress " said Helen at last " how sweet you will look Gladys ".

"Don't be sarcastic" said Gladys with a smile little dreaming how pretty she looked even then in her simple dressing gown.

"Oh I say there is 12 o'clock striking" cried Helen starting up "I've been here a whole two hours, it is really disgracful, well goodnight Gladys dear" she added as she flew quickly out of the room as the last stroke of midnight died softly away.

CHAPTER XXXII

THE MARRIAGE

AT 11 o'clock precisely, as Gladys had said the marriage ceremony began.

Gladys as I have already said was attired in a white satin trained dress made to fit her slender figure to perfection and covered with thin tule. She wore orange blossom in her hair and on her dress and a magnificent diamond crescent caught up her veil.

Helen and Mina Lincarrol were the brides-maids they also wore white. Their dresses were exactly alike, but to colour them a little, they were delicately shaded with primrose yellow; long satin streamers hung from the bouquets they carried and both being dark girls the colour suited them admirably.

The page, a little Spanish cousin of Mulberry's was attired in white and yellow satin

also and very pretty he looked, being just
five years old and very dark with an olive
complexion.

Lionel Lincarrol a tall handsome man of five
or six and twenty gave his sister away as his
father could not come up for the ceremony.

The mighty cathedral was filled to over-
flowing; the most part of the people were
invited guests as Lord Beaufort was very popular
in society; but a great many ordinary people
had just dropped in to try and catch a glimpse
of the bride and bridegroom as they march up
the church.

At last the service drew to a close, and the
guests got into their carriages to drive back to
Portman Square where the wedding breakfast
was to take place.

One of the enormous reception rooms had
been beautifully decorated with sprays of real
orange blossom from Lord Beaufort's hot house
and many other bridal decorations. A magnificent breakfast was then partaken of, every
article being of the highest quality for Mulberry
Beaufort prided himself on never half doing
things.

The guests then repaired to another room to
inspect Gladys's wedding presents, which were
numerous and costly.

And so the day wore on and 5 o'clock found
Gladys, Mulberry, Helen, Mina, Lionel and
Lawrence all at the railway station waiting for

the boat train to take Gladys and Mulberry to Newhaven for whence they were to cross the channel.

Glady's travelling dress was extremely pretty being made of pale blue grey which suited her very well.

At last the train came slowly into the station and the happy pair got in.

The goodbyes were brief and cheerful, good luck being wished on every side.

Mulberry expected to be in London again by the end of Febuary and by that time Helen and Lawrence would probably be one.

At last the whistle sounded and those left on the platform watched the train till it rushed into the tunnel, and then they turned and went on to the opposite platform to take the train for Norfolk.

It was a long journey and they were all tired when they got there.

The brougham had been sent to meet them and though the others all knew the road to their house so perfectly, Helen looked out of the window with a new interest for it was all strange to her.

After a drive of a $\frac{1}{4}$ of an hour or more the carriage drew up in front of a fine old house standing rather back from the road and with a beautiful carriage sweep in front. In the moonlight it presented a very pretty picture.

Before the coachman had time to ring

Lawrence had jumped out and opened the front door.

They then crossed the hall and entered the drawing room a beautifully furnished room.

Mrs. Lincarrol was reading by the fire when they all entered. She was a very tall thin woman with reddy coloured hair done very high on her head and small winky blue eyes. Her features were fairly good, but she was powdered profusely and indeed her hair looked as though it had seen a good many bottles of hair dye. She was attired in an evening dress of purple velvit trimmed with black satin and jet. Helen glanced at her as she rose from her chair and wondered how she came to have such a good looking family. But she quickly became aware that the room contained two other occupants. Two girls were seated at the piano trying some duets. They were both tall and fair with blue eyes and pale complexions and they wore rose coloured dresses. From Gladys' discription Helen knew they were the twins Ethel and Elsie.

Mrs. Lincarrol rose as they entered and having embraced her family turned with a queer look in her eyes to Helen.

" So this is Helen Winston " ? she said holding out her hand, " my niece I think "

Helen did not quite know what to say so she merely smiled and she was then introduced

to Ethel and Elsie, both of whom she liked
very much, especially the former.

"Now I think you'd better go and see your
father" exclaimed Mrs. Lincarrol at last "you
will find him in the library with Hugh, no
doubt Helen would like to make her uncle's
acquaintance".

"I should" replied Helen.

So they all marched across the hall and
opening another door entered the library.

"So here you all are again" cried a cheery
voice from within and at the same moment
a tall well built man came forward. He was a
contrast to his wife in every way, being fairly
stout, dark and brown eyed. He had a kind
though stern looking face. He greeted Helen
very cordially with none of the shifty glances
his wife had made use of and then introduced
Hugh to her. He was only $17\frac{1}{2}$ with dark
hair and eyes and very much resembled Lionel.

"Well I'm glad to see you all back," cried
Mr. Lincarrol, "but you all look tired, I
suppose the journey was long"?

"Not very" replied Minna who had hitherto
kept a discreet silence, "but I'm very hungry.

"Why of course you must be, ring the bell
Hugh" cried Mr. Lincarrol heartily "and I'll
see you get something at once."

"A very good meal was soon brought up
and it was quickly disposed of.

"Well Helen I'm going to bed now" said

219

Minna at last, " if you come now I'll show you your room ".

" Oh thank you " replied Helen and with that they both walked upstairs together.

Lionel and Hugh soon followed their example and so Lawrence was left alone with his father.

" A very nice girl Helen Winston seems ", cried Mr. Lincarrol, " I admire your taste Lawrence ".

" I'm glad you do " answered Lawrence, " I was struck with her when I first met her ".

" Yes I certainly admire your choice " replied Mr. Lincarrol, and after a few more words they both retired to bed.

CHAPTER XXXIII

FIVE YEARS LATER

FIVE years have elapsed since we last saw Helen. Let us choose a favourable moment to view our heroine after the lengthy interval.

Seated in a large and wealthily furnished drawing room by a bright fire, writing at a neat little table, sits Helen, now no longer Helen Winston but Mrs. Lincarrol. The clock had just struck 4. and the shades of the December evening are fast drawing in. By the light of the fire however we can get a tolerably good view of Helen. She has altered but little during the past five years of her

married life. She looks a trifle older, but the
change is so slight as to be scarcely perceptible.
She has still the luxurious black hair and long
lashes shading her soft eyes.

She is clothed in a rich tea-gown of a
delicate green. She is writing diligently and
seems intent on her work but she occasionally
looks up to address a word or two to a
delicate looking little girl of about three years
who is playing on the hearth with a little fox
terrier. This is little Nellie, the only child,
a pale-faced fair-haired little thing, who has
attained her third year today.

At length it grows too dark to see, so closing
her blotter with a snap, Helen walks to the
window and holding aside the heavy velvit
curtain gazes out accross the frost-bitten garden
and the roofs of the houses, which are dotted
about the town of B———.

" Dear me " she says " it is beginning to
snow " I think dear " she adds turning to her
child " it is time you went up to the nursery
tea will be ready I expect."

So saying she rings a bell and Marshland
appears, looking very different to when we last
saw her, in her black dress and clean cap and
apron. Having stuck to Helen in the hour of
trial she now finds herself the much-respected
nurse of little Nellie.

Nellie having departed to the upper regions,
Helen once more resumes her writing, this

time by the aid of a large standing lamp. By
and bye a servent enters with some tea. " Is
Mr. Lincarrol in yet " ? enquires Helen. " No
m'am I think not " replies the servent. " oh
then I shant expect him till late " answers
Helen and so saying she partakes of her tea
alone, which done she goes to the piano and
plays a few merry sonatas. At length the
clock strikes seven, and Helen is about to go
and dress for dinner, when the butler enters
with the message that a woman from the village
of Huntsdown (5 miles distant) wishes to see
her at once on a very important matter.

" Who is the woman " ? askes Helen in great
astonishment.

" I dont know mum " replies the butler
" she is very poor-looking and says she's
tramped all the way from Huntsdown to see
you, but she wont give no name ".

" How extraordinary ! " says Helen, " I know
no one living in Huntsdown, in fact I have only
been there once ; but however I will go and
see the poor soul ". and rising as she speaks
Helen vanishes into the hall.

An old woman of about 60 or 70 is standing
in a remote corner of the hall. The butler had
spoken truthfully when he said the woman was
poor looking. She wears a tattered dress of
some faded hue, and on the top of that a man's
coat, which might once have been black but is
now almost bottle-green. A thin shawl coveres

her shoulders and a battered black bonnet hangs back from her head. Her iron-grey hair is streaming over her face, still damp with the falling snow.

"Did you wish to speak to me" asks Helen kindly advancing to the woman.

"I do mum" replies the poor creature, dropping a bob-curtsey as she speaks. "I've bin tramping from Huntsdown since 4 o'clock and bin nearly turned back by the snow."

"What is your name", enquires Helen.

"Mrs. Cotton, if you please mum" answers the woman," but to get on with my story, you must know I live at "The Jolly Dutchman" in Huntsdown. My husband keeps the inn, but he dont do much bussiness; the place is so remote-like, and I'm afraid he's a bad lot", and here Mrs. Cotton shook her head regretfully "but to come to the point mum, a week or so ago, a poor man all ragged and looking terribly ill, come to the door and asked if we could let him in to sleep the night, as he'd no were to go and no money. My husband was drunk at the time and turned the poor man away in spite of my pleading for him. A few minutes later when my husband was in the bar I opened the door and seeing the poor man there I could not resist letting him in. So according I gave him the attic at the top of the 'ouse, where he has bin laying ill ever since without my 'usband knowing".

"What a sad story" says Helen gently "but I'm sure it was very good of you to risk taking the man in. I suppose you came to me for money did you not"?

"No mum not for that" replies Mrs. Cotton sadly "you see I've tried to save a little money myself during the last few years so I've been able to have the doctor in once or twice to look at the poor man. Mr. Harland his name is. Me and my girl Sally, we've made the attic as comfortable as we can and I've lit a fire up there once, but you see mum coles costs money like everythink else. The doctor say there's not much 'ope for the poor man, he's dying fast of fever and consumption. The other night mum, your gardiner, happened to come in for a glass of something and of course he got talking with the other men and the conversation fell on you mum, and he said he's known you a long time ever since you was Miss Winston (or some such name as that) At the time the talk was going on, I was sitting upstairs with Mr. Harland and as the door was open we could hear the talk in the bar quite distinct ; well mum, directly Mr. Harland heard your name mentioned, he got quite wild and excited all of a sudden and went raving on about you and he would'nt be satisfied till I told him all I knew about you. I *was* astonished mum I can tell you. After that Mr. Harland seemed much quieter and all yesterday and today he's

been in a sort of stupor, but about half past
three today he called me and told me he'd not
got very long to live and would I do him a
favour? I said "Yes", so he told me to go
into the town and ask you to come and see him
at once. He says he knew you quite well some
time back and you knew him too, but you
probably have forgotten the name now. I tell
you mum I was fair took aback, but however
leaving my girl Sally in charge of him, I started
off on my errand, and here I am mum, waiting
to know what your answer may be to this extraordinary request?"

"It is a most extraordinary request" as you
say Mrs. Cotton, and I never knew anybody
by the name of Harland" replied Helen.

"My idea is mum" says Mrs. Cotton "that
the poor man is dilerious."

"Very likely" answered Helen, "but to
please him, I will order the carriage and we
will drive over together, you look far too tired
and cold to walk."

As Helen speaks she toches a spring bell,
and then reaching a sable-lined cloak from the
peg she puts it on drawing the hood over her
soft brown hair.

She then orders a baskitt of streangthing
things to be packed for the invalid.

Then the carriage comes round to the front
door and the two get in. A contrast indeed !
The one small, shrivelled and shrunken,

hugging her wreatched garments round her to keep out the biting cold; the other tall and stately, her rich cloak falling gracefully round her slender figure.

The drive is long and dreary; being for the most a long straight road with tall hedges at either side and an occasional cottage or tree releiving the monotony of the scenery. But Helen, leaning back in her comfortable carriage is not thinking of the passing scenery, but of the extraordinary mission she is bent on.

At length the carriage stops, and Mrs. Cotton leads the way up to a small tumble down dirty looking inn, whith an almost illegable incription painted in white letters, "The jolly Dutchman", Thomas Cotton".

Mrs. Cotton opens the door and Helen finds herself in a very small and filthy dirty passage. A strong smell of beer and tobacco greet her on entering. A door on one side of the passage is half open, and looking through, Helen can see three or four rough looking men seated round a table with mugs of beer before them and pipes in their mouths, and the sounds that issue from the room are none of the pleasantest, for the men are talking, laughing and shouting, not to say swearing.

In disgust Helen turns to the door of the other room. It is a kitchen evidently and a remarkably dirty one too. A candle is burning in this room, and by the light of it Helen can see a slovenly looking girl stirring some horrid smelling stuff in a saucepan, while a very small baby is yelling its heart out in a wooden cradle.

"Here Sally" cries Mrs. Cotton to the girl "how is the invalid"

"No better" replies Sally wiping her hands on her apron "I lit a fire for him, 'cause he grumbled so about the cold".

"I dont wonder at it" responds Mrs. Cotton, "well mum", she continues turning to Helen "perhaps you'll step upstairs, its that door there mum with the handle off", and she points with her grimy finger to a door at the top of the stairs. Helen climbs the ricketty staircase with a wild fear and misgiving at her heart, wondering what the result of this strange visit will be. A light is burning in the room she enters. It is a damp cold place, a trifle larger than the passage below. A miserable fire is doing its best to burn in the grate and judging by the amount of matches strewn about, Sally must have been exerting many patient efforts to get it to burn at all.

The window was minus a pane of glass and the cold wind blew right through the room making the door bang to and fro with a madly montonous tone.

Helen glanced hastily round the room, but the corners being in darkness, she had to hold the candle above her head to see anything at all. In doing so a groan caught her ear and advancing to the corner from when it issued, Helen perceived a sort of pallet bed streached on the floor, covered with a singal blankett. Placing the candle on the floor close by, Helen knelt down and with trembling hands and a quaking heart pulled the covering away. And then——no wonder Helen uttered that low stifled cry; for there with his pale thin face turned towards her and his skeleton hands clutching at the blankett, there with his eyes dim and sunken and his breath coming quick and short lay Cyril Sheene alias Mr. Harland. For a moment Helen could not utter a sound, the words seemed to stick in her throat, and she knelt gazing in horror and amazement at the fast-dying man. It was Cyril who broke the awful silence, "Helen" he whispered brokenly "what a long time you were coming".

"I never dreamt it was you Cyril" answered Helen taking his thin hand in hers, for now all her heart seemed to warm towards the man who had wronged her so much and who was so soon going to leave her.

"No of course not" replied the dying man "you never thought I would come to this —— (here he stopped for breath), "but I want to tell you this before I die".

"Cyril you must not die" cried Helen, opening her basket and producing some wine.

"No, no" gasped Cyril pushing the glass

away "its no use, I know I'm dying, the doctor said so; give me some water to ease my throat and I'll go on".

Helen gave him his wish and then knelt down beside him while he continued.

" After I left you Helen, that day you went to Richmond, I intended going to Picadilly to pawn some things as I had no money to pay my debts. When I got back to my amazement a letter from Mr. Palsey was waiting for me, which explained that the police were already on our track and that if I valued my life I had better leave London and go to some place with him. Of course I had no choice but to go, but oh Helen if you could have known my feelings when I thought I should not see you again. Hastily I scrawled a note to you and added a few lines to my will, you read them did'nt you ? " Helen nodded in assent.

" Well " continued Cyril, " having made my preperations, I started off to meet Palsey. We traveled together. I forget where we were going. Palsey told me how he had escaped after he had been locked up in the drawing room. We had to change at Charing Cross I think and scarcely had we set foot on the platform, when up came two policemen and before we could say a word we found ourselves handcuffed. Well to make a long story short we were tried and I was sentenced to 10 years penal servitude, and Palsey who had done the most part of the crime had penal servitude for life. Well after three years of my time had passed, I was granted a free pardon for saving the life of someone. I have no time to tell the whole story now. At first I was delighted at the mere thought of being free again, but then I recollected I had no friends nobody to care wether I lived or died. When I was set free I wandered about trying in vain to find you Helen. But I got no news of you, untill one day I read of your marriage in the paper. Then I gave up all hope of ever seeing you again. Soon after I fell ill and spent many weeks in an old barn, attended only by a child who used to go messages for me etc : till I was well enough to walk about again. Then my wanderings began again, and I found them harder than ever. After my severe illness I could no longer bear sleeping out. I had to buy lodgings wherever I happened to be, and once or twice when I had no money I had to sleep out in the fields. That did for me Helen. From that day I grew much worse. A young man took pity on me one night and gave me a room in his house for nothing. But with his exception no one cared and so I wandered on untill late one night I arrived at this miserable inn. I did'nt know where I was, but I thought it safe to take another name. So I was brought up here, where I should certainly have died had not some one down in the bar mentioned your name, and then the excitement of seeing you kept me up—

Here Cyril stopped gasping for breath and Helen with her tears fast falling administered water to him and propped up his pillows.

" Helen " cried Cyril at last, he could barely talk now, " do you forgive me ? "

" Oh Cyril " cried Helen " of course I do ; oh if only you had come to me before, how happily this might have ended. I forgive you fully from the bottom of my heart."

Cyril smiled, he was too far gone to talk and Helen could see his eyes growing brighter.

A long silence followed while Cyril's breathing grew laboured and slow. Presently with a great effort he turned and caught Helen's hand in his own. " Helen I'm going fast. Goodbye I die happy since you forgive me." And Helen stooped and kissed him. He turned and looked at her for the last time and then his spirit passed quietly and peacefully away.

CHAPTER XXXIV

CONCLUSION

A year has passed since the sad events recorded in our last chapter, and Cyril has long been laid in the church yards sod. His grave is ever bright with flowers placed there by Helen's loving hands and by those of her children Nellie and John.

Of Mr. Palsey little has been heard but it has lately been rumoured that he died a natural death in prison, though some people exagerate and say he died by his own hand.

Marshland is still living though her health is gradually becoming weaker.

And what of Helen herself?

Let us look into her drawing room to-night and we shall see her once again.

It is New Year's Eve and the drawing room, hall, rather spacious rooms are all lit up, while the many happy people are dancing and enjoying themselves. For Helen is giving a dance. Yes, a gathering of all her oldest and dearest friends. Among the many faces we recognise the Lincarrols. Even *Mrs*. Lincarrol is there gorgeously got up in bright yellow silk which she is proudly telling everybody was the foundation of her grandmother's wedding dress.

Minna and her husband (for she is now married) are both there, also Ethel who is engaged and Elsie who has just returned from her honeymoon. Lionel is the only one not there, but he is doing well in America.

Hugh (now in the Army) is also attending the dance. But Gladys where is she? She is also there with her husband Lord Beaufort and while the latter is talking to Lawrence let us notice Gladys who is deep in conversation with Helen.

Seated on a sofa close to the entrance of the green-house, idly watching the dancers as they waltz round the spacious room, we once more see Helen and Gladys in close companionship. What a pretty contrast they make !

Helen with her dark hair as abundant as ever and the lovely colour on her cheeks.

She is glancing down and her long lashes cover her eyes. She looks very happy and a smile is playing about her lips.

She wears a pale violet coloured dress made in the latest fashion and the colour suits her to perfection. Gladys is attired in white silk trimmed with bright gauzy ruffles of pale pink and silver. She is playing with her fan and laughing merrily with Helen. Her bright blue eyes are full of happiness and a little colour has come into her usually pale cheeks.

"Ah well Helen dear" she is saying "you have nothing to grumble at now I'm sure."

"I never said I had" laughs Helen, "I am perfectly happy with Lawrence and my children and it *is* so nice to have you here again, but all the same I have had troubles ; a good many more than most people of my age."

"Yes that's undeniable" replied Gladys "but still you have a dear husband and lovely children."

"Of course I have" cries Helen "and I am quite happy now."

"And as far as I can see there is no reason why you should ever be unhappy again," replies Gladys.

"No" says Helen, "but still I cant quite forget the sadness of my early years."

"Nonsense my dear," cries Gladys, "dont forget what you told me so long ago about your sorrows, they will become like wounds which though healed over are still to be seen, and so though you will not exactly forget the sorrow you will no longer feel the pain."

"Yes" answers Helen laughingly, "that was a very good idea on my part; and though applicable to you then, it certainly applies to me now.

So now our story comes to an end and we will bid goodbye to Helen. She has already partaken freely of the cup of sorrow but now her time has come and she knows what true happiness is and all her sorrows, miseries and heartaches shall be blotted out in that sea of mist and shadows ;—The Past.

THE END.